Dedalus Origi

Market Farm

Nicholas Bradbury was born in Lagos, Nigeria, where his father worked as an architect. From the age of four he grew up in Yorkshire and later in Warwickshire. His career has encompassed government, banking and public relations in England, Canada and Hong Kong. He now lives with his wife and son in Oxford.

Market Farm is his first novel.

Nicholas Bradbury

Market Farm

(or How the Foxes Broke the Piggy Bank)

Dedalus

Supported using public funding by
**ARTS COUNCIL
ENGLAND**

Published in the UK by Dedalus Limited,
24-26, St Judith's Lane, Sawtry, Cambs, PE28 5XE
email: info@dedalusbooks.com
www.dedalusbooks.com

ISBN printed book 978 1 909232 23 5
ISBN ebook 978 1 909232 55 6

Dedalus is distributed in the USA by SCB Distributors,
15608 South New Century Drive, Gardena, CA 90248
email: info@scbdistributors.com   web: www.scbdistributors.com

Dedalus is distributed in Australia by Peribo Pty Ltd.
58, Beaumont Road, Mount Kuring-gai, N.S.W. 2080
email: info@peribo.com.au

First published by Dedalus in 2013
Market Farm copyright © Nicholas Bradbury 2013

The right of Nicholas Bradbury to be identified as the author of this work
has been asserted by him in accordance with the Copyright, Designs and
Patents Act, 1988.

Printed in Finland by Bookwell
Typeset by Marie Lane

A C.I.P. listing for this book is available on request.

based on a true story

"Money mediates transactions; ritual mediates experience, including social experience. Money provides a standard for measuring worth; ritual standardises situations, and so helps us to evaluate them. Money makes a link between the present and the future, so does ritual. The more we reflect on the richness of the metaphor, the more it becomes clear that this is no metaphor. Money is only an extreme and specialised type of ritual."

Mary Douglas (via Will Self)

Acknowledgement

Many people have encouraged me in life, and my wife and son, as well as friends, continue to do so. Some people have also given small but important encouragements to me in relation to writing, especially Gianni Celati, Saul Bellow and Margaret Atwood. All deserve my thanks, while the latter deserve my apology for having put off the task in any seriousness for far too long. For his great help with moving this work to publication, and his other kindnesses to me and my family over many years, my deep appreciation goes to Adam Williams. Finally, my gratitude goes to Jüri Gabriel and Dedalus for their bold decision to back an unpublished writer.

Preface

You may know of *Animal Farm.* The animals overthrew the farmer and his men and set up their own farm. They thought they would be free. But the pigs, and in particular those led by Napoleon, took over. After that, things did not work out well at all for most of the animals. In fact, things turned out even worse than was recorded at the time.

It was not the only farm to undergo a transformation, however. There was another farm where the animals overthrew the farmer and established their own rule. They too thought they would be free. Yet in the end, things did not work out well there either, although in a different way. In fact, things will turn out worse on this farm than many of its animals suspect. They call it Market Farm.

Contents

Running Free

It was a quiet day on Market Farm. The pigs, inclined as usual to laziness and good living, were to be seen wandering about the yard before sauntering off to the Farm House to enjoy a convivial afternoon discussing just how well everything had gone in the past year – indeed in the many years since they had taken over. Chickens scratched for corn, the sheep lay in the fields and the horses went about their labours diligently but unhurriedly, while the cows wandered obediently to the cowsheds for milking. Even the dogs, who had in the distant past been objects of fear on the farm, had grown fat and indolent as the largely trouble free years had gone by.

Not every day was so well ordered, nor the work so easy. By and large, however, life was accepted by all those on the farm for what it was. It could be better, but it could be worse, and the stable life and the quiet contentment had led to easy-going relations among the animals of the farm. Nowhere was this more apparent than in the friendships that had grown, which may not have been likely in earlier ages.

Just such an association had arisen between three animals who had in recent years become the firmest of friends, Merlin, Erroll and Lily. The trio were taking a leisurely stroll, chatting of this and that, when the subject turned to the Farm Council. The farm was managed on behalf of the animals by the pigs through the Council, which held its meetings every week in the Farm House and for which elections were held every four years. Although all of the pigs held rather similar views on what was good for the farm, there were sufficient divergences of opinion for two groups to have taken shape over time. These became known as the blues and the pinks, following the colours they wore at election time.

Merlin was a greying donkey who often said little. When he did, he was often accused of cynicism – though to his mind, he merely saw things as they were and expressed himself accordingly. So it was today.

"Blue and pink, it's all the same," said Merlin, in his usual flat, emotionless tone. "Whatever group is in charge, the farm goes about its business. And of course the pigs make sure that they are well rewarded for not getting in the way too much."

Undeniably, the pigs reserved a portion of whatever was produced on the farm for their own use, to nourish their all-important brains, by means of the Annual Tithe, which produce was stored in the great Tithe Barn near the Farm House. But as they pointed out, this tithe was also used in many other ways beneficial to the farm and its animals. It was used to feed the dogs who were to guard against intruders; to store up grain in case the harvest failed; and to trade with the Great Outside, to buy things that the farm itself could not provide.

Lily ruffled her feathers at Merlin's criticism. She was an innocent young chicken, kind hearted and always ready to think good of any animal, though usually quite timid in her views and actions.

"It's only natural that the pig should manage the farm's affairs and hold sway on the Farm Council, they're clearly the cleverest and most articulate animals," she said, as if repeating a mere commonplace. "I know some animals question whether it's right that they should do less of the physical labour than we other animals do. But I think that their work, the brain work I mean, and telling the farm animals what to do, must be very taxing. I could never do it. I think it's much more difficult and important than building or ploughing or hoeing or sowing or reaping. Any animal can do those."

Erroll agreed, after a fashion. He was a strapping bullock just entering his prime, full of the energy and optimism of youth, and never afraid to express himself or to leap into action.

"The pigs are farm animals just like us, so they must have the best interests of Market Farm at heart. In any case, the most important point is that all of us animals, from the largest to the smallest, are free – free from tyranny," he bellowed, aping one of the rhetorical flourishes sometimes used by the pigs.

Indeed it was true. Freedom, not tithes and produce, was what Market Farm was all about. Freedom was what had been fought for long ago, and the animals' triumph over tyranny was symbolised by the Freedom Tree, a gnarled old oak which had been the site of an important battle in which the animals had wrested control of the farm from the ancient rule of humans in a tide of revolution. Above it hung a carefully carved plaque that proclaimed "freedom for all".

It was beneath this tree that the occasional "Freedom Meetings" were held, where any animal could get up and air his or her views on any subject. This, at least, was the theory, although in practice, the pigs insisted on a more orderly agenda. Otherwise, as they said, matters could "slip from hoof and trotter", and chaos would surely ensue.

The Freedom Tree was thus one of the most important things on the entire farm. As long as the Freedom Tree still stood, it was said, no animal would again have to "bow down and give of his produce to corrupt overlords who labour not but live off the fat of the land". Although the language in which this sentiment was expressed now had something of an archaic ring to it, it remained at the very core of the animals' sense of what made Market Farm their home.

Even Merlin was inclined to agree with this sentiment. "Yes, whatever else, we must never forget the freedom we enjoy, which is not the anarchy of the wild animals beyond the farm fence, but the free association of a community of animals all working for the common good. As for the pigs, for all their faults, we will never forget how they led the fight for liberty. And nor will they, I hope."

Foxes!

It was a measure of how secure the animals of Market Farm felt behind their fences and hedgerows, and with a Farm Council led by good stout pigs, that when foxes were sighted near the farm, there was no immediate alarm. After all, foxes had been part of farm life – or more precisely, farm death – since time immemorial. Their numbers were always few, and they lived always beyond the pale. So the animals kept a watchful eye on their borders, but otherwise went about their business very much as usual.

At the Freedom Meetings, the older pigs especially sought to reassure the animals on the farm that they were perfectly safe.

"We give you our solemn promise that never shall foxes be allowed to harm any farm animal," said Bluffer, a portly, avuncular figure who was the leader of the "blue" pigs who currently dominated the Council and hence was the leader of Market Farm itself. "As pigs, we have gained your trust through protecting Market Farm from danger, and we will never betray this trust. We will work tirelessly to ensure that you will continue to lead lives free of worry and strife."

The animals were much relieved to hear the pigs make their position so clear. Yet the sightings of foxes, after a short lull, seemed gradually to increase. And one day, a young goat named Terry announced that he had seen some of the younger pigs talking with foxes near one of the hedgerows. "They looked like they were friends," he told an assembled crowd in a voice trembling with adolescent excitement. All the animals laughed, this observation merely reinforcing the general opinion that goats were among the least intelligent of animals, wild or ruralised. No wonder the expression "sorting the sheep from the goats" had arisen!

It was not long, however, before the animals were shocked to discover that the observation had perhaps been right. For one week shortly afterwards, a small group of foxes was seen actually entering the Farm House, escorted by some of the pigs! Moreover, they indeed appeared to be on cordial terms. There was consternation at the farm, and great debate as to the significance of the event, which every animal was sure would never be repeated. Yet repeated it was, with foxes coming and going, albeit discretely, ever more frequently and seemingly in ever closer conversation with the pigs.

At the Freedom Meetings, the animals demanded an explanation.

"How can you pigs even think of meeting with the foxes! What good can possibly come of it?" brayed Cynthia, one of the mares, shaking her flaxen mane in outrage. "Are you going to give them the freedom of the chicken run?"

Not surprisingly, at this inflammatory suggestion, the chickens, Lily among them, set up a tremendous clucking and flapping of wings, soon joined by a fervid quacking and hissing from the ducks and the geese, who felt only slightly less menaced at the thought. The cacophony was deafening, and even some of the pigs, stout as they were, had thoughts about calling on the dogs, just in case.

But Bristle, one of the livelier and younger pigs who had been most instrumental in inviting the foxes to the farm, rose and motioned for silence. "The world changes, things move on," he said with smooth self-assurance, and casting his eyes over the crowd of animals beneath him. "We need to keep open minds and to seek the truth, examine the facts. We need new ideas. New blood. Something to rouse us from our slumbers. Are there better ways of running Market Farm? Could we be even freer? More prosperous? It's no good just sticking to the past in everything we do, my friends. Talking to the foxes is just a part of the process. We would be failing in our duty to you as pigs if we did not explore every opportunity to improve your lives. There is nothing to fear, my dear animals, but fear itself."

Whether by force of argument, or rhetoric or from simple confusion, Bristle's words had the desired effect. The clucking and flapping subsided, and somehow the meeting ended with agreement that the ideas could be explored, provided that the sanctity of the chicken run could be guaranteed inviolable.

So the visits of the foxes continued, and despite a lingering fear, the longer the foxes were present on the farm, the more the animals got used to these distant relatives. This acceptance was very much helped by the foxes' well groomed appearance, their impeccable manners and their articulate way of speaking, which made a deep impression on the animals of Market Farm. So provided the foxes kept their distance, and did no harm, the animals were not inclined to demand that they leave. In any case, if needed, the pigs would surely turn to the dogs to chase the foxes out.

Eventually, several families of foxes moved onto an unused hill in a large field at the edge of the farm behind the Farm House, where they built houses surrounded by thick, high holly bushes and entered by a narrow gate above which hung a sign that said "Vegetarian Villas" in large lettering.

Land Reform

Sure enough, along with the foxes came the new ideas that Bristle had talked about. Small improvements were made to many aspects of the farm, which eased the animals' workloads a little and promised better harvests. New drainage channels were dug, gates repaired and crops "rationalised", to use a new word the foxes introduced to the farm vocabulary.

"Freedom is good. Freedom purifies. But the proof of the value of freedom is the turnips in your troughs, the hay in your mangers and the seeds in your trays. The foxes will bring more of these to us. It's going to be a brave new world for all of us!" explained Bristle at another of the Freedom Meetings, where he was an ever more vocal figure.

"Bravo! Bravo!" bellowed Erroll, whose fiery optimism had made him one of the most enthusiastic supporters of the "new breed" of pigs who were now pushing for "rationalisation".

Nor was he to be disappointed. The foxes' first initiatives were just the precursors of a much more radical change – land reform. One of the greatest barriers to progress at the farm that the foxes had identified, according to the pigs who had discussed things with them, was the ill defined nature of who owned what. The animals were surprised, since they thought they knew very well what belonged to whom, and that at the end of the day, all the animals owned pretty much all that was on the farm. But it was explained to them that here was a much broader question that, once solved, would unleash slumbering productive forces to the great benefit of all.

"We are proposing, that for the good of Market Farm and all of its animals, we carry out without delay a root and branch reform of the present system" announced Bristle in Council one day, shining with greater confidence than ever, "No longer should we countenance our backward ways, with animals simply wandering aimlessly around the farm, unfairly sharing field and food. This is a goad to idleness and living off the efforts of others. Henceforth, let each animal's share in the farm be defined exactly, bounded by rights that guarantee their freedoms. Let the fields and buildings be parcelled out, to each animal according to his need and ability, and let each animal use his talents to make the most of what the farm has given him."

Not surprisingly, given the radical nature of what was proposed, there was much debate in the Farm Council, and much bargaining. But in the end, as always, a compromise was reached. As insisted upon by the "blues", an appropriate portion of the disbursement was reserved for the foxes, for their role in devising and implementing this revolutionary new system. But as equally firmly insisted on by the "pinks", a sizeable amount was also to be kept in common for all the animals to enjoy and for future enterprises of common endeavour. And of course, appropriate portions were to be given to each and every pig, whose contributions to the farm were, they all agreed, collectively beyond measure.

When these reforms were announced at the next Freedom Meeting, the animals were hesitant but also excited by the prospect of actually owning not just their own feathers and hides, and small possessions, but plots of land also. Certificates were drawn up and each animal received their own in a great ceremony held under the Freedom Tree. The certificates were very prettily drawn and, moreover, were written with the most impressively grave and precise sounding language that the animals had ever encountered. The animals also knew, or rather had been told, that they were very valuable, and would one day allow them to live a life of plenty and ease, without the need to toil in the fields.

Erroll was especially enthusiastic. As soon as he got his certificate, he stampeded over to Merlin, "Here we go!" he said, waving the paper in the air and tossing his young horns with delight. "It's going to be a new life for all of us! Who knows what might happen, or how things will change!"

"Who knows indeed," said Merlin, his voice tinged with customary melancholy.

As the weeks and months went by, however, some of the animals felt a touch of disappointment at their certificates. Their lives had not changed at all as they had hoped. Every animal went about his work in much the same way as before, the old social relations affected not one jot by the beautiful new certificates.

In many ways, this suited the foxes very well. For it was not long before a trade in the certificates began. The animals who could see no immediate use for them were easily persuaded to give them up in exchange for food or pretty objects they had long coveted, and although they were not the only animals to suggest such an exchange, the foxes seemed among the most prepared to do so.

Those animals who sold felt themselves straight away to be richer and more fulfilled. This helped foster a growing sense of acceptance by the animals of Market Farm, not merely of the certificates, but of the newly arrived foxes, who indeed appeared to be increasing the sum of animal happiness.

Although most animals held on to their certificates, as much from lack of understanding as anything else, few indeed, could see any point in the foxes exchanging real things for mere pieces of paper, especially when they often involved "rights" to hilly land, scrubland and land far away from the best pastures. Every animal on the farm knew these areas to be virtually worthless and were secretly pleased that the wild foxes' ignorance of the fundamentals of farm life had led them down the wrong path.

Besides, one thing that comforted all the animals, was that a good portion of the best land had been reserved as common land. Here the very young and the older animals could rest, enjoy the sunset and even scratch for food. Like the great Tithe Barn, the common land provided a sense of security against the eventuality of disaster, and was hence perhaps even more important than the reserves which the pigs claimed to have stored for years of lean harvests.

Lily herself was very tempted to exchange her certificate.

"I have always wanted to have a little box in which to keep my things, and there was such a nice one offered to me by a very handsome young fox only yesterday," she told Merlin, apparently oblivious to the fact that she had been able to remain in the company of a fox with complete equanimity.

"Be patient Lily," Merlin cautioned, shaking his grey old head, "Think about it. If the animals who thought up this scheme want more of the certificates, they must have a reason. Remember, the farm doesn't belong to all of us anymore, not as a herd. In any case, you don't have many things, do you?"

So Lily thought and thought, this way and that, but the more she thought, the less she had any idea what to do.

Nose Rings

To liven things up further, and to make the exchange of certificates easier, a second major change was instigated at the farm – the introduction of nose rings. The foxes had by now been accepted into the fold and they explained that the animals' manner of sharing from a common trough, or rooting around for food across the fields and pastures in haphazard fashion, occasionally bartering among themselves for the things they wanted, was no longer possible following the Land Reform. So the foxes had persuaded the pigs to set up a new system in place of the barter the animals had all been used to.

When the animals had taken over the farm, long, long ago, to mark their new-found freedom, they had all turned in their nose rings. It was proposed that these nose rings would be used as a means of exchange, which would allow the animals to buy and sell their possessions and labour as freely as they pleased. Almost overnight, therefore, the nose rings turned from a hated symbol of human oppression, to symbols of the freedom each and every animal would henceforth enjoy to live life as he or she pleased.

The nose rings were taken to a room in the Farm Forge. The room was closely guarded by two of the fiercest dogs and only a very select group of pigs was allowed in, accompanied by some rabbits. On pain of banishment, no other animal was entitled to enter. Here, the rabbits polished the nose rings and inscribed them with the words "freedom" around the rim, in such carefully designed letters that no other animal would ever have the skill to copy them. Henceforth no animal was to use any other object for the purpose of exchange. And they would all be stored in the great Tithe Barn, where surplus produce had from time immemorial been stored against harsh winters.

But another problem presented itself. "We must find a good way of keeping them all safe," said Bluffer. "Even the barn might not be safe enough."

The pigs thought and thought, curling their little tails tighter and tighter as they did so.

"How about a wooden chest, of the sort that was used to keep blankets for the winter?" suggested Bristle, "With some good padlocks."

"Not a bad idea," conceded Bluffer, swaying his great chin from side to side. "But perhaps we also need something symbolic, something that would give our animals full trust in the arrangement. As you know, they won't understand the idea at first. Well, none of us are really sure about it, if truth be told."

"I know," said the ambitious Bristle, "You remember how the farmer used to keep his money in a little model pig. A piggy bank it was called. Why don't we use one of those?"

The idea was so flattering to the pigs' sensibilities that it was immediately agreed upon, and a large piggy bank was made, with a slot in the top just the right size for nose rings, and a mechanism in the tail that acted as a lock. The piggy bank would keep the nose rings safe as safe could be, and for extra safety, it was put right in the centre of the Tithe Barn. Because of this, and in reference to its importance, it was christened the Central Piggy Bank.

The nose rings were introduced at a specially arranged Freedom Meeting. Their shiny appearance made an immediate impression on the animals, who were entranced by the lustre of the nose rings, which seemed to promise so much happiness and hope for the future. It was also explained at the meeting that the animals would now receive nose rings in return for the work that they did, and that they would be able to use the nose rings to buy what they wanted. Such freedom of choice would bring boundless happiness, the pigs assured the assembled, echoing the views of the foxes. As wise old Bluffer had predicted, the idea of the Central Piggy Bank was also very successful, as the thought of the farm's traditional leaders and guardians also guarding these new magic rings gave an additional sense of security to the animals.

"This will be a milestone in the development of Market Farm," said Scratcher, a fiery sow among a band of younger pigs who were becoming increasingly vocal at the Freedom Meetings and on the Farm Council. "Every animal is now freer than ever before to work as he or she desires, to buy what he or she wants to buy, to be what he or she wants to be. This will lead to freedom and prosperity such as we have never before dreamed of. It is the dawn of a new and fabulous era in the history of Market Farm!"

The pigs reserved a large portion of nose rings for safe keeping in the Central Piggy Bank in the Tithe Barn and distributed the remainder through groups of foxes. They set up huts made of straw which they called "counting houses" in the yard in front of the Farm House, each with a counter, as well as their own smaller piggy bank, in which the nose rings were kept. Although it was a confusing and at times painful transition, the whole organisation of the farm changed remarkably quickly, and the animals soon became used to visiting the straw huts, where they could keep their nose rings safe and take them out when needed, with everything neatly recorded by the foxes on little wooden tablets, all for such a very small fee that they hardly noticed.

The animals who had ended up owning the larger plots of private land following the Land Reform – principally the foxes and pigs – offered to pay those who owned little – the sheep, cattle, horses, ducks and chickens – to work the land for them. Indeed, these animals had no choice, since the common land would by no means support them any longer.

This suited Erroll just fine. He was a strong young bull and hard work was almost a pleasure to him, giving him as it did the chance to show off his power. He put his every sinew into clearing land and pulling the heavy equipment needed for tilling, and generally helping in every way he could. And he was pleased at the end of each week with the shiny nose rings that he received. So too was Lily, who never imagined that helping with weeding, as well as laying eggs, could have led to the accumulation of little piles of shiny nose rings, which could be used for such a variety of things.

For the new system ushered in by the Land Reform and the nose rings had made the land much more productive, with not only more being planted but more of each crop ripening and being harvested. More interestingly from the animals' point of view, the growing also became more specialised, as the owners of land tried to produce different foods that they might be able to sell.

The change in the way that food was produced in due course led to an explosion of shopkeeping. Merlin was one of a number of goats and donkeys who had huts in which they sold not only grains and turnips but the new vegetables that were now being planted. Most rented these little buildings from the pigs and foxes, but Merlin, who had quietly made a few exchanges in days following the Land Reform, owned a little hut of his own. He had even taken the bold step of displaying some items from the Great Outside that he had brought into Market Farm in exchange for some of the farm's produce. This proved a shrewd move, as the rarity of these items, combined with the increasing abundance on the farm, allowed him to charge a great deal more than he paid for them.

So, just as the foxes had predicted, there was both more abundance and more variety, to the animals' great contentment.

"I can't believe just what there is to buy!" exclaimed Lily, who had tied a pretty pink ribbon in her feathers, which made her feel younger and more beautiful than ever before. "And I've seen the loveliest mirrors that I want to buy, so as soon as I've saved up enough nose rings, I'm going to get one all for myself."

"You know what, Lily," said Erroll, "I've just tasted the best piece of corn I've ever had. I bought it from old Nellie's shop. Say what you like about the foxes, they've brought nothing but good since they arrived. And Nellie told me that she was expecting to have all sorts of new produce later this year – even purple potatoes. Purple potatoes! Can you imagine? What about you, Merlin, what have you bought?"

Curiously, Merlin, despite being a shop owner, was little interested in buying things except to sell them. "Not much," he replied. "I don't have many nose rings yet. But one day I'll buy myself some nice things. You might also want to save a bit. You never know what will happen."

"You're always so gloomy Merlin. You've got to learn to enjoy life more!" boomed Erroll, shouldering the donkey in a friendly way. "You only live once."

"Most probably true," said Merlin, but he was not to be moved and unconsciously dug his hooves deeper into the turf.

The Teachings of Old Erasmus

The foxes had clearly been the instigators of the far-reaching reforms that had increased the prosperity, though also the divisions, at Market Farm, and had gained some measure of acceptance. Even so, both they and the pigs sensed keenly that the new regime was not altogether accepted. But Scratcher hit upon a brainwave – or perhaps the brainwave simply hit him, or perhaps it had dawned upon her over the course of her many conversations with Blink. "We must draw upon Old Erasmus," she told Bluffer at one of the Inner Councils.

Old Erasmus was a pig of great learning and insight who had lived over a century ago. He had shocked the entire herd by suggesting that far from being a creation of the Almighty Boar who had existed since before the beginning of time, the farm animals as they now were had come down in a direct line from wild animals who lived in ages gone by, and that as a result, they shared an ancestry even with those they despised or feared in the forests and mountains that lay in the distance beyond the farm gates. In other words, the animals of the farm were actually close relatives of the foxes!

According to Old Erasmus' theory – at least as told by some of his descendants – the success of an animal in life was determined not by the good graces of the Almighty Boar but by Mother Nature. She, "red in tooth and claw", demanded the fiercest competition of animal against animal and it was this that drove the herd forward. Each animal vied with brother or sister to secure a particular place in the natural order of things.

This theory of "Mother Nature's Bounty", as it was called, was utterly abhorrent at first to the majority of the animals. But it gradually became accepted by many of them, although some still insisted that the Almighty Boar was ultimately responsible for the birth of Mother Nature and had individually designed the animals and the plants in all their detail. Mother Nature must have a cause they argued, just as an egg must be preceded by a chicken, and surely no creation as perfect as a pig, or even a goose, could simply be a random event. The Almighty Boar must somehow have used his divine trotters to shape the clay from which all animals were made.

In any case, even those animals who accepted the logic of Old Erasmus, nonetheless firmly insisted that what made the farm the farm, and the wild the wild, was precisely the fact that in the farm, this raw and war-like spirit had been tamed. Certainly, Old Erasmus himself had never suggested this arrangement of Mother Nature was a virtue to be followed by the animals in their day-to-day interactions.

The foxes saw it differently, however, insisting that freedom meant exactly this, and arguing that "going against Nature" could only lead to untold miseries. And the longer the foxes, despite their distance from the community generally, remained in place, the more this interpretation of Mother

Nature's Bounty seemed to be applied to the farm's everyday life, rather than to the march of the ages. Scratcher recognised that this was a powerful argument indeed, and would solve the divide that still existed between the foxes and the farm animals.

"Life is a struggle of individual animal against individual animal, and we must all work together as individuals against each other to ensure that our farm remains free and prosperous," she said at one of the Freedom Meetings. The chickens and sheep, at once frightened and uplifted by this confusing statement, sent up a loud clucking and baaing, before the speaker continued. "We must recapture the spirit of the ancient animal world before even the rise of farms, from our untamed ancestors, who were lean and swift and bold, cunning fighters, heroes in every sense of the word. The more we act as they did, the freer we will be and the more Mother Nature will reward us with her bounty."

"But surely, this is the cry of the foxes!" cried a young mare. "Already, the foxes live well and seem to run ahead of every other animal in the farm, though they joined us much later. How can the sheep and the chickens outrun the foxes?"

This thought, that the foxes might use their speed and cunning to take a greater share of what the farm produced caused a shiver to run down the spines of even some of the pigs, who lately had begun to feel the pressure of vying with their smaller, wilder cousins. Bristle immediately rose again to allay the fears.

"The foxes, fellow animals, are our friends and have helped to create the greater prosperity we all now enjoy. Do not forget that. Do not forget also, that we, you, all of us are freer than any animals ever in the history of animal kind. Why can a chicken not apply herself, and one day become a vixen?

Why can a ram not learn to become even better than a fox? Everything is possible in this world, which is now the best of all possible worlds. There are no limits to what you can achieve. All you need is application, self belief and to study hard, and your dreams will come true!"

As if on cue, Bristle's supporters among the pigs began an approving chorus of grunts, which was soon echoed by the bleats and cackles of the sheep and chickens, who once more had hope in their hearts, and a spinning in their heads.

The Invisible Snout

The foxes' peculiar interpretation of the theories of Old Erasmus undoubtedly had its genesis in a long-held religious conviction of their own, the cult of the Invisible Snout.

"Each animal must give according to his abilities, and receive according to the needs of the Invisible Snout." The foxes felt that this motto should become the central credo for all the animals of Market Farm. Ultimately, it was this belief that would underpin the industry of the community, and create a fair and just system of effort and rewards. Though it might rarely be grasped or talked about, unlike the slogans about freedom, it was important that it permeated the animals' souls, for their good and the good of all the farm.

Quite what the Invisible Snout was, few animals, even among the foxes, really understood. It was, after all, invisible. Since ever more of the pigs appeared to have taken up worship of the Snout – while the foxes seemed convinced of its ability to work miracles – by and large the animals all accepted that the Snout was a good thing, an aid to freedom and prosperity. Only through its mysterious movements would the farm prosper and remain free. So it was paramount for the freedom of the animals of the farm that the Snout should remain free to weave its magic.

Of course, there were some troublesome animals who occasionally questioned whether the Snout was or should be as all powerful as the Almighty Boar, and whether the animals themselves should not attempt to control its snuffling and shuffling, which seemed always to leave the pigs and foxes with relatively more, and the other animals with relatively less. But it was noticed that animals who were suspicious of the Snout were generally less well rewarded than those who were fervent believers. So when any animal suggested chasing the Snout out of Market Farm, a fear almost akin to panic arose and instead, the heretic was beaten and himself run off the farm, dragging his tail behind him.

To underline the importance of the Snout and its workings to the farm, and the heritage, as they saw it, of Old Erasmus, the pigs decided to make more apparent the exact significance of the slogan adorning the Freedom Tree. So the old plaque with the simple phrase "freedom for all" was replaced by a new one, which read "freedom and prosperity for all".

In truth, the new phrase seemed to sum up the new reality of Market Farm, and so no animal uttered so much as a bleat or a squawk when it was changed. Yet despite the increasing abundance, the animals did not benefit equally. The pay of the animals who worked in the fields owned by others was only loosely related to the amount they produced. Most animals felt that they were now working harder than before, which somewhat offset their new freedom to choose where to work and what to eat. Moreover, a small but persistent minority, unable to find much work, now spent their time on the common land, scratching a rather bare existence.

This was especially true of many older animals, and at one Freedom Meeting, Scratcher even gave his opinion that such animals were "no longer pulling their weight" and that "something would have to be done".

"Every animal, through hard work, has an equal chance to put as much food in his or her belly as any other," Scratcher continued. "Simply giving an animal food only encourages him to fail to realise his potential, doing him no good at all and creating a millstone that hangs around all our necks."

This unleashed a debate among the animals, from which Lily, Erroll and Merlin were not excluded. Lily was a tender-hearted chicken and felt sorry for these unfortunate brethren. She would even give them some food that she had spare on occasion.

"It's not as if it's their fault," she explained to Erroll. "After all, we're all going to get older one day, and what if we get sick? Won't the farm look after us?"

"You're wrong Lily," countered Erroll, exercising his broad shoulders as he spoke. "I agree sometimes there's a real reason, but often they're just lazy. I know you're a good chicken and you want to help, but like Scratcher says, charity will only encourage them in their sloth."

Lily was never entirely sure about her opinions when challenged, no more so than when one of her closest friends was the source of disagreement. "What do you think, Merlin?" she asked.

"Does it really matter what I think? You really should learn to trust yourself more, Lily."

The Factory

The new farming methods introduced by the foxes seemed to work well, and as much of the produce was now traded with farms not just in the neighbourhood, but even further afield in the Great Outside, a sense of luxury arose, especially among the pigs, who could now savour delights that were not found on Market Farm, such as peaches and lemons and even pomegranates. Their freedom of choice was greater than ever before, and even though most of the animals were able to enjoy only a very small addition to their diet, they nonetheless had to agree that, as Bluffer so eloquently put it, they'd "never had it so good".

The foxes, however, were not content with the progress. In his occasional secretive meetings in the Farm House with the senior pigs of the Inner Council, Blink (a fox whose mind was reckoned to be so fast that he could think of an answer before most animals had even thought of the question) waxed lyrically about farms in the Great Outside that were so abundant in arable land, where production was ever so much higher than even the new model farm they had helped to create, that every animal lived a life of happiness, and the pigs basked in the glory of the prosperity they had created.

The pigs were intrigued, and Blink seized the moment – as he always did.

"To give but one example, the chickens of Market Farm are not laying anywhere near as often as they could," he explained, narrowing his eyes and looking at Scratcher and Bristle for support. "And believe me, this would be easy to improve upon. You wouldn't believe what a little investment can do. To be honest, what we've done so far is just the beginning. We need to rationalise the production of the whole farm much further. So let's begin with eggs. What we need is a factory. A chicken factory."

So plans were drawn up and the field near the old chicken coop was cleared. The chickens clucked loudly that their land was being taken away. "But that's our field!" said Lily, running with wings flapping to confront Scratcher, along with several of her friends.

"My fellow animals," said Scratcher, "you must remember that this field has never truly been yours. Even in the old days, it was mere custom that allowed you to use it, and custom is not a right. And during the Land Reform, it was made clear to each and every one of you that this asset was to be held in common for the benefit of all in the farm, and should therefore be used to maximise the benefit of all the animals."

This did not satisfy the chickens, who did not know what an asset was but did not like the idea that their beloved field was to be turned into one. They began to run around frenziedly, and set up such a clucking that it was not long before other animals began to come and look to see what was going on.

Many clearly sympathised with the chickens, not least because they feared that their customary grazing would one day suffer the same fate.

So Bluffer was called. Despite all the reforms, Bluffer was still far more trusted than the likes of Bristle or Scratcher, and hence remained the public face of the pig's leadership of the farm.

"Do not worry, my dear chickens," he said, his portly face beaming with sincerity. "This is progress. This is freedom. A new life of even greater riches awaits you. A fraternity of pigs and foxes has paid a high price for the land – nose rings which will swell the coffers of the Tithe Barn. And the land will house a new factory – a factory which is designed to benefit you. Yes, you chickens. And as soon as it is finished, you will all be able to live and work there. The rickety old coops in which you now live are being cleared away and soon you will be living safe and warm in a climate-controlled environment. The factory will be more efficient and you will happily be able to lay more eggs. And with demand for eggs high, you will be among the richest animals in Market Farm."

A factory! The news that the farm was going to get a factory caused great excitement among the assembled animals, and even Lily and her fellow chickens began to see the possibilities. So the protest died away and before long lorries arrived with piles of equipment and material.

Erroll was hired to help with the construction, and could not contain his enthusiasm not only for the nose rings he was being paid, but for the fact that he was helping to build a new life for his friend, Lily.

Finally, the great day came and the factory was opened. The gleam of the metal and the energy of the construction work already seemed to speak of a bright future. All the chickens,

Lily among them, were ushered into the new building. Indeed, Lily had to marvel at the newness of it all, and especially the lights, even if the rooms they were to occupy seemed rather cramped, with almost no room to spread their wings. However, over half of the rooms were empty and after all, she had long since forgotten how to fly. "Perhaps after all the factory will be more convenient than those rickety old coops, where we were all forced to share one big room," she thought to herself. "And the coops were cold and draughty in the winter." So there she sat, and there the other chickens sat, row upon row, laying as never before.

Sadly, however, some of the chickens found themselves unable to lay fast enough, and soon lost their place in the factory. Instead they sought to earn some corn-money by performing dances and other special services in darkened little sheds at the back of the farm's outbuildings, often paying a proportion of what they earned to some of the more aggressive roosters to protect them from the attentions of other aggressive roosters.

Playing Dominos

It was not so very long after the introduction of the nose rings that the freedom of the animals was soon expanded even further by the skill of the foxes.

"You've seen, my dear pigs, the great things that the nose rings have done for the farm," said Blink. "Every animal is much better off and I'm sure there's never been this much activity on the farm. But the nose rings are heavy and cumbersome. And they're not easy to make. What we need is something less solid. What we need is nose rings made of paper. They'll be so much more convenient!"

"I promise you, you won't believe the effect it will have upon the farm, or," he added with a winning smile, "how popular it will make you."

The pigs could see no flaw in this argument and so readily agreed at the next Farm Council meeting that paper nose rings should be introduced, to the benefit of all. The rabbits were, for all their timidity, surprisingly clever animals and had done so well in polishing and stamping the nose rings. So the pigs saw no reason why they should not be entrusted with the paper version.

The rabbits thought about it very carefully and made some pretty rectangles of paper stamped with little dots in the amount of a certain number of nose rings. Merlin, well known as being from a breed of very stubborn animals who often had quirky ideas, remarked that the front of the notes looked rather like some of the dominos that they used to play with on the farm. So from that day on, the paper nose rings became known simply as "dominos". The foxes were given dominos representing exactly the number of nose rings in their piggy banks, and before long, while the piggy banks were full of nose rings, the business of the farm was conducted entirely in dominos.

Once the dominos had been firmly accepted by the animals as symbolic of the nose rings, which were in turn symbols of the wealth of the farm itself, the foxes argued that even greater wonders could be achieved if the supply of dominos could be increased. "It's all very, very straightforward," explained Blink, slowly moving his tail from side to side. "After all, there would never have been enough nose rings to go round to satisfy every animal's wish. But with dominos it's a different matter. Think about it. In theory and in practice, the rabbits can easily write out as many dominos as required to make the farm go round faster. And this means that we can safely lend out dominos to animals who need them, to help them exercise their freedoms even more. I can assure you that we will be more than helpful in this regard."

So one fine day the pigs announced that the foxes, "out of the goodness of their tender hearts", would be prepared "on behalf of the animals and for the good of the farm," to lend dominos to such animals as needed them.

"This is a marvellous development that will over time change the face of Market Farm and bring to life in the best possible way the full meaning of freedoms that it has always stood for," Bristle announced, his short hairs almost rigid with the excitement of it all. "From now on, no one need go unfulfilled. Every animal can borrow dominos to buy land or sheds or food. It will usher in an even brighter new era of prosperity."

Indeed it was true. All any duck or goose or sheep had to do was to promise to pay the foxes back the amount borrowed later on, plus a little bit extra each month. To this effect the animals would have to sign a note of hand with "IOU" written in big letters at the top. On the back of the IOU, which many animals did not bother to read, there was some very small writing saying that until that time, the foxes were the owners of whatever the dominos had bought.

Since the new dominos would only increase the production of the farm, all was to the good. In effect, the inevitable future increase in prosperity was merely being brought forward to today. What happiness for the animals!

"What a wonderful idea!" said Lily. "Now I'll be able to buy those ribbons I always wanted."

"Lily, you must be careful," cautioned Merlin. "Remember, you'll need to pay the dominos back one day."

"No problem!" exclaimed Erroll. "Since the new factory opened, it's easy for Lily to make more dominos. All she has to do is lay more eggs."

"Yes that's right Erroll. Oh Merlin, you're such an old stick-in-the-mud," Lily said with an affectionate sigh. "What's the use of all this freedom if you're not going to use it." And she rushed off to one of the foxes' huts to see how many dominos she could borrow.

Not surprisingly, it was not long before the foxes had to ask the pigs to tell the rabbits to draw some more dominos, so that they could lend these out. The pigs obliged. Nonetheless, on the advice of the rabbits, who (not without reason) were very nervous creatures, they insisted that the nose rings in the foxes' boxes should be in proportion to the dominos and IOUs, just in case something (they weren't quite sure what) went wrong.

Furthermore, it was felt that to make sure all went well, the whole system would need proper supervision. It was decided that the rabbits, who had done so well in designing the dominos in the first place, would be the best animals for the job. Most animals felt that the rabbits were an excellent choice, given their quick movements, their careful diet of lettuce and their ability to hop over obstacles, smell danger from afar and run quickly to fetch help if necessary.

"And above all," said Scratcher, "we need animals with real 'teeth', to make sure that the foxes and everyone else stay in line. And rabbits' front teeth are, as every animal knows, even bigger than those of foxes!"

So it was that the rabbits, led by a Chief Rabbit named Benjamin, whom the pigs had appointed, were put in charge of both the Farm Forge and the Central Piggy Bank. Benjamin was sworn in at a ceremony under the Freedom Tree.

Benjamin and his fellow rabbits were charged with making sure that the foxes behaved, and were told to be very tough indeed on any fox who went against sound principles in the matter of dominos and IOUs. This meant that the foxes should be careful that the IOUs they had received would always be repaid in full and that for every five dominos lent out, a fox must have at least one nose ring safe in his padlocked box. To help the rabbits in this task, they were given a brand new printing press, which would allow them to print new dominos when needed, rather than laboriously write them out by paw.

With complete independence from the pigs who appointed them, and particularly (for obvious historical reasons) from the foxes, the rabbits were thought to represent the interests of the entire body of animals without favour – perhaps even more than the pigs on the Farm Council. In particular, much faith was placed in the Chief Rabbit, who once a month would appear in Council and give a little mimed performance about his work during the period. The pigs, with their enormous size, and the foxes, with their very sharp teeth, were pleased enough with the arrangement.

The few animals who were brave enough to make use of the extra dominos early on did well, as they were able to increase their holdings in the farm way beyond their immediate means.

Erroll was one of these. He borrowed as much as he could to buy a large stall for himself, which he then set about making comfortable, sealing up cracks that let the drafts in, polishing the wood and adding some nice fresh bales of hay.

He invited Lily and Merlin for a stall-warming party and the friends enjoyed a pleasant evening with some very nice elderberry wine, one of the many new kinds of drink that were becoming popular on the farm.

"It's so lovely Merlin!" clucked Lily approvingly. "To think, Erroll, you have such a wonderful stall all to yourself. And it's so smart and comfortable. You really are the envy of the farm!"

"Don't exaggerate Lily. I'm hardly the envy of the farm. It's nothing like the Farm House, or Vegetarian Villas. I've never been there myself of course, but I hear from those that have that they are the most amazing places, with all kinds of luxuries," Erroll replied. "But I am happy. It's a fine place to live and do you know what, it's worth a bit more now than when I bought it. I've half a mind to save up more and buy another one."

"What on earth for?" asked Lily.

"Why to rent out of course. Like Merlin does."

"Merlin! Are you really? But you're always so sceptical about everything! Don't tell me you're signing IOUs as well?" Lily asked, incredulously. "In any case, you're still living in that little shed of yours!"

"It's quite comfortable and it suits me well enough, Lily," said Merlin. "Perhaps one day I'll think about something a little bigger. But only when I feel safe."

"Safe, what do you mean, safe?" laughed Erroll. "Things have never been better. There's no way that anyone's going to attack the farm, not with the foxes inside the gates already. What could possibly go wrong?"

What indeed, thought Merlin.

Given the small fortunes that were being made, it was not surprising that over time, more and more animals joined in and before long, borrowing dominos and signing IOUs became a part of the everyday life of Market Farm.

Indeed, the pigs themselves soon became among the most enthusiastic proponents of "staking a claim on the future", as they called it. They would use IOUs drawn very prettily with nice pictures of the Tithe Barn to borrow considerable sums of dominos from the foxes, who collected them on behalf of the other animals. The pigs would then use these dominos to pay the animals in turn to work on useful improvements for the farm, such as the digging of new irrigation channels. Since these "T-Barns", as they were called for short, were backed by the "full faith and credit" of the pigs, who collected the tithes, they had to pay back to the foxes rather less than the amount which the other animals were obliged to pay. Not surprisingly, the T-Barns proved a strong temptation and over time, came to account for the greater proportion of all the IOUs in Market Farm.

For all the good things that the IOUs brought, as usual there were some tiresome voices warning that pieces of paper were only pieces of paper and nothing good would come of this alchemy. It was also clear that the more the farm became dominated by dominos, the wider the gap became between those animals who had many and those who had few. Yet such voices were crying in the wind and dismissed as mere throwbacks to a primitive past. Since the prices of land and other items such as the woods and quarries were only ever increasing in value, every animal was said to be happy. It was, as Scratcher put it "a win-win situation".

Quite how "win-win" the arrangement was in reality was soon open to doubt, however. With dominos and IOUs being created in great numbers, but the supply of land necessarily limited, it was not too long before prices began to rise sharply and a fever of speculation engulfed the land and buildings of Market Farm, as every animal sought to improve his or her lot through buying and selling as much and as quickly as possible, in a game called "flipping".

There was almost always a distinct hierarchy to the exchanges. First, the chickens sold something they all knew to be of little value to the foxes. The foxes liked to buy when no animal was looking, and since they now had the complete run of the chicken factory, such deals were often concluded in darker corners of the building at dusk, when the sky was grey and animals were feeding.

The pigs then got wind that the foxes had found something very valuable, and since they admired the foxes' judgement, began to buy from the sheep, albeit at higher prices than the foxes had paid. Then the goats bought from the geese and the horses from the cows, and so on down the line. When prices finally reached an almost vertical peak during a frenzy of buying and selling, the entire round went into reverse, starting with the foxes, who sold back to the wildly clamouring chickens. Needless to say, the chickens did not even remember having sold to the foxes in the first place what they were now buying back from them. Lily was in this respect lucky in that she was so timid and indecisive that by the time she made up her mind to join in, it was already too late.

The animals were amazed to see so many fortunes made – or so few, if they had been counting more correctly. Only two types of animals rarely joined in the merry-go-round: the rabbits, who were too nervous, and the donkeys like Merlin, who were too stubborn and, according to most of the animals, far too cynical. Both of these curious animals carefully acquired whatever nose rings they could lay their hands on and stored them underground, occasionally buying little sheds or parcels of land in popular parts of the farm which they could use to grow food or rent to other animals for their needs.

Puppet Shows and Entertainers

The Farm Council meetings were held in the great Farm House, and only the pigs elected onto the Council each year could attend. The Freedom Meetings were therefore an important way the other animals could make their views heard and find out what was going on.

The pigs would also offer a daily circular from a stall in front of the Freedom Tree, the Pig Times, which in a rather dry and sober manner would give the animals notice of the important events of the previous day, and a summary of the latest Council speeches.

Then the foxes created their own circular, written by some rabbits they employed for the purpose. This contained mainly the prices of every conceivable item on the farm, with reports on why they were "up" or "down". It was called the Fox Times, and was written on special russet coloured paper. But although the foxes found the numbers it contained of the highest importance, it was little read by the other animals, who found it numbingly boring and of absolutely no bearing on their lives.

Merlin read it, of course, but he was well known as an eccentric, even by the standards of donkeys. Lily would tease him about it.

"Why Merlin, you're such a dry old stick already and if you read any more of the Fox Times, you'll become so dry not a leaf will grow on you! There's nothing in that scribbling that you won't see better by taking a walk through the farm."

"That may be truer than you know, Lily," admitted Merlin. But he kept to his reading all the same.

It was inevitable, however, as the farm got busier, and life became more diverse, with the profusion of different types of roots, vegetables and fruit on offer, and all the activity of buying and selling, not to mention the borrowing of dominos, that the animals would begin to seek their own sources of information and entertainment.

The foxes, ever eager to help, obliged them. They began to employ other animals, called "entertainers", to produce circulars which "spoke to their own kind". These circulars often contained as many drawings as words and had titles in big letters for the animals who had difficulty in concentrating. They focused more on the everyday lives of the animals than the dull facts of the Farm Council meetings or the numbers of turnips produced. There were often stories about the love lives of the pigs, and glamorous (if highly fictional) evocations of the lives led by the foxes in Vegetarian Villas. Many of the stories were wildly speculative, such as reports of a duck who could honk like a gander, a bull who was producing milk, or a perennial favourite – a prediction by a little chicken that the sky would fall in the following week.

Perhaps precisely because of the often inaccurate yet highly colourful nature of these circulars, they became wildly popular. Before long a fierce competition raged among the Daily Cow, the Evening Quack, the Baaa and the News of the Chickens to attract the most readers, with ever more exaggerated reports of both what had happened the previous day, and what had not. The animals referred to them as "the rags", knowing that they had to take them with a pinch of salt, but they loved them all the same.

To add to the appeal of the rags, the most ordinary animals were asked by the entertainers to express their views on the important matters of the day, such as whether the harvest would be good next year or which pig should lead the Farm Council. Many a chicken, duck and sheep was quoted, talking confidently about every issue.

"This is very important," said Bristle, rubbing his head against a post. "It's important that the will of the animals is expressed openly and freely, so that they can feel that while we – that is while you – bear the onerous responsibility of running the farm, it is they who are the true masters."

Indeed, it gave a warm glow to the animals to see their own kind represented in the circulars. But what was actually said by them was largely ignored, since it was well understood that their views could not be very clever or very informed. Only the pigs and foxes really knew what was going on, the animals suspected, but they were not entirely to be trusted. It was a bit of a conundrum.

Yet even the simple circulars were beyond the patience or understanding of many of the animals, especially the chickens, whose interest rarely went beyond the titles, and the sheep, who often merely stared at the pictures. Lily was enthralled especially by the pictures of exotic fowl and their fine plumage, which she found in the especially colourful weekend editions.

Instead, many chose to go to one of the "puppet boxes" that had rapidly been set up, where some of the more intelligent animals acted out the stories of the day using a combination of mime and glove puppetry. To the delight of the animals, these puppet shows made the dull reports of the circulars seem so much more real and immediate. As with the entertainers, the puppeteers would even invite animals on to perform their own mimes, for others to enjoy, in a display of "reality puppetry" as it was called.

With so much information so conveniently available, and the animals able to express their opinions freely via the rags and puppet shows, the foxes began to question whether the Freedom Meetings were any longer of use, or of "utility" as they preferred to call it.

"The trouble with the Freedom Meetings," Blink explained, in one of his ever more frequent conversations with Scratcher at the Farm House, over a rather fine bottle of wine that he'd brought over, "is that they're not really free. Think about it, most of the animals don't even bother to attend. And with those that do, it's often just a small group of troublemakers. You know the ones I mean. The goats and the donkeys and the like. They're forever nannying and braying and asking difficult questions. They just dominate proceedings at the expense of the silent majority. It's this majority that is now being given full voice, in the rags and puppet shows."

Scratcher and the pigs were easily persuaded by the logic of this argument, which would indeed make running the farm much easier, or "more efficient" in the foxes' jargon. So it was decided that the meetings would be abandoned, and that animals wishing to express their opinions should instead use the "proper channels", and write them down, putting them in the suggestion box at the Farm House, for due consideration by the pigs. These, the pigs assured, would be debated with due seriousness at the Farm Council and reported in full in the Pig Times and, accordingly as the writers wished, in the rags.

Not surprisingly, the cancellation of the Freedom Meetings led to weeks of bleating and lowing and cluck-cluck-clucking. At one point, the pigs even began to doubt whether there might not be some real trouble over the issue. But in the end, nothing happened as the animals were busy with their everyday lives. The energy of the protests dissipated and before very long, the Freedom Meetings faded into memory.

The process of gentle forgetting was, by a curious twist of fate, aided by an increase in the amount of "news" made available to the animals. To make the spread of information even faster, a particularly enterprising young goat had hit upon the idea of enlisting the thousands of sparrows that lived on the farm to spread what they had read or heard to the animals. The sparrows could remember no more than fifteen words at a time, but would gaily fly from animal to animal, happily twittering fragments of unconnected stories. Despite, or perhaps because of, the disjointed and rather meaningless nature of these fragments of stories, they became extremely popular. In fact they became popular to the point where the animals would become filled with anxiety if a sparrow had not perched on their shoulder for as little as a minute, fearing that they were missing some vital item of farm news. Never before had the animals had access to so much information! Indeed, they were so bombarded with it they could escape it only with great will and imagination – attributes which very few of them had.

The foxes were very pleased with this state of affairs. "It's just as we thought. A real triumph! The free flow of information is what freedom is really about and it's the very foundation of prosperity," said Blink, whose coat seemed shinier than ever under the spring time sun. "Look how much freer the animals are than they ever were before. Now every animal has the opportunity to gain the fullest insight into the workings of Market Farm. They're empowered to make their opinions known and to know the opinions of others. It's this that gives them energy and the drive to work even harder and to increase their prosperity, which is, after all, what life is all about."

Scratcher took this idea up in slightly different terms in a speech in Council that was repeated, to a greater or lesser extent, in all the puppet shows.

"Truly it is an age of freedom. Today, all is known and nothing is unknown. There are no more unknown knowns, nor are there unknown unknowns. This has made every animal not only truly free, but truly equal, since each and every animal has an equal opportunity to use his or her freedom to achieve the prosperity they desire and deserve. We are living on the best of all possible farms!" she thundered, her steely little eyes surveying the assembled pigs.

When she had finished, the pigs responded with one of the loudest and most extended oinkings.

Many of the animals, however, felt that they understood even less than before, as the abundance of incomplete and often contradictory "bites" of news whirled like a snowstorm around them. Others, by contrast, felt they understood absolutely everything without having to even think about it, and for exactly the same reasons. Neither group reflected much on the fact that all of the puppeteers and entertainers, despite the apparent diversity, were paid for their efforts by the foxes, nor that the fine speeches by Scratcher and Bristle might reflect opinions not entirely formed in their own porcine brains.

The Agronomists

The rag writers and the puppeteers had a voracious appetite for "news", as they called it, and with the farm animals ever more in the thrall of speculating on land and buildings, they became the ideal venue for a group of foxes who called themselves "the agronomists".

These foxes believed themselves to be the most ardent acolytes of the cult of the Snout, and claimed to be able to see its mysterious movements in the patterns of the clouds, the flight of the crows, the rustle of leaves in the trees and through making arcane connections – or "correlations" – between the profusion of numbers printed in the Fox Times. They would, for a fee, use their special powers to utter oracles and divinations for those animals seeking to know how the Snout would bestow or retract its favours.

Nor was this entirely illogical. The harvest from the seed sown today is dependent on the vagaries of the future that would decide how the seed would grow tomorrow, and hence any fox who through divine intercourse with the Snout could gain insight into its workings, would be worth a great deal of corn indeed. So over time, such punditry became among the most important and well paid of all the activities on the farm. The agronomists were paid vast sums to predict the coming of the rains and the size of future harvests, or where the next barn might appear, or how many dominos an acre of land might be sold for, two seasons hence.

Of course they could do no such thing, and although some undoubtedly were more accurate than others, this was in no greater number than the rolling of a dice would have predicted. The more honest among them knew it, although the more arrogant believed their uniquely sensitive ears and bushy tails were proof of their divine ability. Remarkably, the more ignorant or unlucky agronomists were able to maintain this belief in spite of the fact that, on average, they were demonstrably more often wrong than right. Nor was this failure of any consequence among the animals at large. Just the slightest chance of the oracles being right was enough for the lucrative punditry to continue. And the more the other animals were stupid or desperate enough to believe in the agronomists' mythmaking, the better, from the agronomists' point of view.

Of particular interest to the agronomists was the Chief Rabbit's nose. Since the rabbit was now central to overseeing the flow of dominos, and since a rabbit's nose was the equivalent of a pig's snout, it was logical to conclude that the Chief Rabbit's nose in its official capacity must resonate here on earth with the ethereal workings of the Snout. As a result, a great deal of the agronomists' time was spent in divining the oracular import of the various twitchings of this particularly pink and fluffy appendage.

Paradoxically, the myth of the agronomists' occult faculties was even strengthened by the fierce theological debates they engaged in, which showed that they could not agree on anything. They argued over the propitious direction of the wind, whether a crow's flight had truly been straight and the exact meaning to be accorded to the slightest sniffing of the Chief Rabbit. Although, in the joke of the day, agronomists were so productive that two agronomists would always produce at least three different opinions on any given subject, the confusion all added to the aura of mystery surrounding the divination process, which simply made the animals clamour for more.

Furthermore, the agronomists' disputations were food and drink to the puppet masters and rag writers, who would eagerly entertain their audiences with appropriately simplified versions, which even the silliest chicken could understand, usually rounding off with very practical advice, such as "buy" or "sell".

Yet this again created a great paradox, for this free flow of apparently enormously diverse opinion from the agronomists, that was served up daily by the entertainers and puppeteers, led to an even greater herd instinct among the animals than that to which they were in any case inherently prone. For the most obscure reasons, the animals would all of a sudden flock to one particular agronomist, and simultaneously follow his divinations. Then, all of a sudden and for no apparent reason, they would lose faith in him and turn to another, and on and on. This led to a constant stampeding into and out of certain areas of the farm or buying of certain types of barn or crop, sending prices soaring and plunging without rhyme or reason.

It was almost only among the foxes themselves, it seemed, that an individual could buy in anticipation of the dramatic rise, or sell before the equally dramatic fall, in prices. Whether this was because they were indeed able to make more accurate predictions of the future than the farm animals, or whether it was because they knew in advance what the agronomists would say, was open to dispute. Fortunately, however, it was not a dispute that was even given more than cursory attention on the farm, busy as the animals were. Even more curiously, it was not unknown for an agronomist who had made a prediction in one direction to nonetheless bet his dominos on precisely the opposite outcome. Indeed, this was very often the case, if truth were told, which it never was.

The Harvest Pie

One of the most amusing and lucrative activities of the agronomists was to try and guess the size of the Harvest Pie.

Each year, in late celebration of the harvest, at the turn of the year, a great pie would be baked in which every animal would share, at a party that lasted a day and a night. The ingredients for the pie were carefully saved from a constant proportion of every crop that the farm produced throughout the year. The circumference of the pie was measured each year by one of the rabbits. The pie was then shared out among the animals, apparently in proportion to how much their work had added to it during the year.

The pie was thus symbolic of the bounty that Mother Nature and the Invisible Snout had given to Market Farm during the year. Since each year it had indeed grown bigger, just as the pigs and foxes had predicted, it was thought right to celebrate not so much the pie's baking as the announcement of the result of the measurement. Indeed, as the pigs never tired of saying, it was of absolute importance to every animal that the pie grow bigger and bigger each year.

Quite why this was so, even now that most of the animals had more than enough to eat, was never made clear. Perhaps even the pigs themselves did not know, but the mantra had been so long repeated that it had become one of the firmest articles of faith for almost every animal in Market Farm. Only the occasional goat would openly question the need for a bigger pie, and such assertions would immediately be greeted with uncomprehending laughter, not least from the sheep, who always felt themselves to be far superior in understanding to the goats, with their suspiciously small horns and daintily cloven hooves.

After many years of reform, the pie was a handsome sight, and even the most circumspect of animals had to agree that there had been a general rise in abundance. When it came to the sharing, however, some of the cleverer animals could not fail to notice that the slices allotted to the foxes and pigs had grown not only in absolute terms, but greatly so in relation to the shares accorded to the other animals. Indeed, it was suspected that the portion of pie that some animals received had actually begun to shrink!

Since most animals were now working harder than ever to produce milk and eggs, carrots and potatoes, ploughshares and buckets, while all the foxes and pigs seemed to do was to shuffle pieces of paper, this hardly seemed just. Indeed, it seemed to some of the animals that some of the foxes and some of the pigs were looking more and more alike. The keener of the pigs appeared to be getting leaner and acquiring a glossier skin. And was it the animals' imagination, or were their snouts getting more pointed? While some of the foxes, such as Fat-tail, had become more corpulent, and their pelts had thinned, and – again was it pure fantasy – their noses appeared to have flattened a little?

However, those who questioned this state of affairs were forcefully reminded that it was the very dominos that were ultimately responsible for all the production of the farm, since it was these that provided the real energy and incentive to work. The swirling of the dominos, they were told, was the closest that could be achieved to making visible the mystery of the Invisible Snout.

Yet however much they scratched their heads, the ordinary animals just could not follow this line of reasoning, and they concluded that perhaps only the truly well educated, such as the foxes, who surely understood the intimate workings of the Snout itself, were really in a position to judge.

Cleaning Up

With so much activity on the farm now, and so many animals, the farm was not only crowded, but it had begun quite frankly to stink.

"I think it's a disgrace," said Lily, who was out with Merlin and Erroll for one of their walks, which because they had all become so busy were much less frequent than they had been. "The air on the farm used to be so fresh it was a joy to be alive. I remember clearly how in the spring we'd have the scent of the cherry blossom and in the autumn we'd smell the ripening wheat, from almost every part of the farm. Now you really have to pick and choose where you go."

"It's true," said Erroll, for once not brimming with optimism on the subject. "It seems that waste, of every kind, has grown along with the increase in produce and population, and our methods for disposing of it just haven't kept up with the scale of the problem."

"It's worse than that," continued Merlin sombrely, as he

kicked a rotting cabbage to the side of the path. "Have you noticed how the pigs have tried to solve the problem? All they've done is to move the cess pits and the rubbish tips and the night-soil collection sites to new areas of the farm. And of course it just so happens that they're all far away from both the Farm House and Vegetarian Villas. Not in their backyard, it seems, is the answer as far as they're concerned."

"Yes!" said Lily, who for once seemed to have developed firm opinions. "And they stay away from these areas as much as possible. And when their duties do require them to go there, they take along pomanders and such like, which they use to ward off the foul smells."

Indeed, Slick, another keen mind among the foxes, had foreseen the problem that the accumulation of rubbish and excrement would bring, and had early on invested in a pressed-flower-making machine for making perfume that was now hugely profitable. "This simply proves that every challenge is also an opportunity," the entertainers said, "it proves that with hard work and a little thought, every problem can be solved and every animal can become rich." And the animals were forced to agree that his idea was very clever, and they kicked themselves – some literally so – for not having had his prescience.

Lily in particular wondered why on earth she had not thought of the idea, because she had lately become so enamoured of these perfumes that she would spend a small fortune in dominos every month to buy a little bottle – a small fortune that all added to the already very large one that Slick had accumulated.

The animals who lived near the tips tried to complain, but were encouraged, if they found the smells unbearable, to move to other parts of the farm. However, as a result of the policy of "waste segregation", prices in the less affected parts of the farm had risen steeply, while those of their own dwellings had fallen. Furthermore, their incomes remained small. So they had no choice but to resign themselves to the situation.

The trouble was that as time went on, the rubbish piled higher and the stink increased in intensity. Even more worryingly, some of the chickens, cattle and sheep living near the middens began to fall ill with mysterious flu-like symptoms. The older animals and the younger ones were especially vulnerable, and there seemed nothing any animal on the farm could do to help.

So a group of ordinary animals – for this is how, by curious chance, they had begun to see themselves – was organised to go and air their grievances. Lily, Erroll and Merlin were among them.

Since there were no longer any Freedom Meetings, they decided to assemble in front of the Farm House. As the large crowd of animals assembled, there was a buzz of excitement such as had rarely been seen in recent times.

"Dear pigs, dear pigs, let us come in!" cried the animals in unison.

Not by the hair of their chinny-chin-chins would the pigs ever let the animals disrupt the hallowed sanctuary of the Farm House, of course. Yet they recognised the strength of feeling on the issue and so Bristle was sent out to "consult" with the crowd.

His stride as he walked through the Farm House garden was confident, but he had taken the precaution to ask some of the farm dogs to follow at a distance. He cleared his throat.

"My fellow animals," he intoned. "As your duly-elected swine, we are acutely aware of the problem. We are entirely sympathetic."

"So what can be done? Now clearly it would be absurd to

reduce the amount of waste being produced. If we reduced the amount of waste created, this would reduce all of our prosperity. The Harvest Pie would not grow! I ask you, where would that leave Market Farm and all of us living in it?" It was, of course, merely a rhetorical question, and as he sensed that in a breach of etiquette a donkey near the front was about to make a retort, he quickly took up the thread, silencing a discontented murmur among the assembled.

"But we do understand that something needs to be done, and needs to be done quickly! And as you know, we are not just pigs who can talk, we are pigs of action! So things will be done to hide the problem better, and to reduce the stench and malevolent odours. Things will be done to make sure that the children of Market Farm grow up in an environment that is clean and healthy. It will take time, but I give you my word as a pig whose only wish has been to serve his farm, that work will begin not next year, not next month, not next week, but tomorrow!"

Although the animals were not entirely happy, it did sound like a start, and so with some reluctance, and to the relief of Bristle and somewhat to the disappointment of some of the dogs, the crowd shuffled off home.

True to his word, the very next day Bristle made an announcement in Council on urgent measures to tackle the problem of waste.

"What we are proposing today is an urgent, effective and far-reaching scheme to tackle the problem of waste. In the coming weeks, I will appoint a special joint 'tusk force' of pigs to investigate what might be the most appropriate solution to the issue. The tusk force will be funded by a special tithe, levied on the production of vegetables. The force's first action, once the problem of its composition and constitution is solved, will be to create special sub-committees to examine every aspect of the matter at hand. These will commission research and then make recommendations to the tusk force on which aspects of the issue should take priority. Once these parameters are established, further committees will be set up to look in detail at how each aspect should best be tackled. These recommendations will then be passed back to the tusk force, which will then establish further committees to examine the budgetary aspects of the recommendations..."

"In the meantime, I will also be offering assistance, drawn from the common trough, of a free pomander a year for those most affected. The details of this scheme will be drawn up by a committee which will be established in due course."

It was a long speech, as befitting the importance of its subject and the radical nature of the proposals. But it ended with some simple and practical advice, which very soon became the main focus of the rags' and puppeteers' reporting of it.

"Pending the resolution of these bold initiatives, I would urge our fellows to move away from the cesspits if they are able to afford it, and to hold their noses if not."

The Fat of the Land

Hoof-in-paw with the problem of muck, was the problem of the fattening of the animals. Fattening was traditionally thought of as something the animals had been forced into by their human masters in the days before Market Farm had thrown off the yoke of their tyranny. Yet now, the problem had returned and with a vengeance. Try as they might, the animals simply could not stop eating.

The abundance which the farm now enjoyed, although not evenly spread by any means, gave most of the animals more than enough to eat. True, for many animals this meant a monotonous diet of rather poor quality, highly processed fodder, worse in some ways than the rough but honest fare of the old farm. But the processed food was livened up by the foxes – who seemed to think of everything – through enriching it heavily with sugar and salt and oil. And so potent was this combination that animals of many descriptions were increasingly inclined to gulp it down by the bucket load.

This was especially true for the younger animals. The frenzy of work on the farm and the need not to "fall behind" in the accumulation of paper had led many animals to abandon their young in order to work even harder. For some this was because they desired more of the exotic feedstuffs and trinkets that were daily paraded before them by the more well-to-do. But for most it was because otherwise, they would rapidly have been unable to pay for daily necessities. So instead of carefully rooting around for the most nourishing food for their lambs and calves and chicks, at the end of the day they would quickly run to collect a bucket of quick meals for the family to eat before bedtime. Even Erroll and Lily would occasionally indulge in such temptations, though Merlin tended to stick to traditional foods, even such as thistles, which had long gone out of fashion.

In a curious twist of fate, however, the diets of the more successful animals remained by and large not unhealthy, while becoming ever more exotic. Black carrots joined the traditional orange variety, small purple sweet potatoes vied for attention with the large brown lumps that were the staple, and every manner of bean, grain, vegetable and fruit from all over the world, as well as cheeses, milks, eggs, cakes and all manner of delicacies, from truffles to morels to nuts and even to chocolate were available.

Erroll had developed a particular taste for Chinese pears, while Lily was fond of prettily-coloured Indian corn, even though it was not, she understood, from India. Even Merlin bought these foods on occasion, and seemed in fact to favour the most unusual and expensive.

"Why, it's so against your nature," Lily remarked to him one day, as she fiddled abstractedly with a little glass-bead necklace she had acquired. "You eat such plain old-fashioned stuff normally!"

"There's no contradiction, Lily," he replied, swishing his tail meditatively from side to side in a slow rhythmic movement. "Or perhaps, the nature of animals is always contradictory." Paradoxically, the more varied the food, the more demanding the animals, the foxes and pigs in particular, became. Turnips were not merely served in a bowl or on a plate (for the more prosperous animals had long since abandoned buckets and troughs) but were now required to be carved into attractive shapes to be admired before eating. The geese, who for some reason seemed the best at preparing such food, competed fiercely with each other to see who could create the most elaborate designs.

They began with relatively simple representations of objects of beauty around the farm, such as flowers and blossoms. But before long, the competition had driven creativity to such heights that no self-respecting fox or pig would deign to eat anything that was not presented as a tower of virtuoso filigree work. To make the spectacle even more dramatic, these delicate, almost ineffable slivers of food were presented on the most enormous plates, as if to emphasise just how unimportant was the actual nourishment involved.

How the animals marvelled at these skills – especially those (meaning the vast majority) unable to eat such wonders themselves! Puppet shows of carrot carving became wildly popular and over time, some of the geese became stallholders and their little eating places thronged with important pigs and foxes. The cleverest among them even became modestly prosperous in their own right.

The abundance of eating eventually led, however, to the Great Fattening. Among the pigs, in any case genetically predisposed to a certain corpulence, were some who began to swell well beyond the normal size. But they were among the least affected, as many animals simply became fatter and fatter. Horses who had once been sleek and able to run like the wind around the meadows now loped along dragging heavy bellies. Many of the chickens, who now sat in the factory for the entire day rather than running clucking around the farmyard, became so bloated that when they tried to run, their legs broke under them.

Nor was it only the vast increase in eating that was to blame for the fattening of the Market Farm animals. Though some still tilled the fields and engaged in the manual work that kept the farm productive, most had now moved into the much more exciting and potentially lucrative business of playing dominos, or tending to the needs of the paper-shuffling pigs and foxes. Their sedentary lives, combined with an increase in the intake of feed, inevitably led to expanded waistlines.

Even Erroll's fine young body had begun to suffer. He too was forever writing IOUs and chasing the latest story, in order to boost his hoard of dominos. As luck was with him, it was allowing him to do less of the physical work he used to engage in. Almost imperceptibly day by day, but ever more visibly month by month, his strong muscles acquired a veneer of fat, his belly sagged, and while he could still run, he was sometimes shorter of breath than he should have been.

Lily had almost the opposite problem. Ever since buying her first mirror, all her happiness and joy had come from the pleasing little changes she had made to her personal appearance. Even her natural plumage no longer satisfied her, and like many of her fellow chickens, she had taken to going to a hut where she could have them dyed the most marvellous colours. Purple was her latest fad, though "not too much, you understand, just enough to ensure an elegant but intriguing sensuality" as her stylist, one of the ducks, explained. So little did she have left over after spending on these decorative enhancements, and so concerned was she to retain her figure, that if anything, she became thinner than before, to the point, her friends warned her (to little avail) that she would do well to eat more.

Young Bloods

The lack of space, of parental attention and the poor diet were having a damaging effect on the young beyond that of growing fat. With little by way of guidance or entertainment, and goaded by the knowledge that they would never be able to enjoy many of the elaborate delicacies the pigs and foxes enjoyed, which the puppet shows laid before their eyes every day with unremitting vigour, they became restless and violent. Groups would assemble, and dreadful fights broke out between rival gangs, with the kids and the lambs becoming among the most aggressive.

Many of the animals tried to avoid such gangs, but they sometimes became targets anyway, and were badly mauled. Often, the violence was fuelled by the habit more and more of the animals had got into of sniffing glue from tins that were stored in the barns. Such substances were supposedly under the strict control of the pigs, and the glue was only to be used for its original purpose as an aid to building and repair. So great was the sense of release from care and frustration that the glue offered, that a dark trade in glue tins had sprung up, that even the dogs could not counter.

Many of the adult animals, for whom the recent abundance of food appeared as an unmitigated blessing when compared to the leaner diet of their youth, found nothing to sympathise with in this delinquent behaviour. "They just need a good whipping, like the farmer would have given!" was Meryvn's view. Yet others had only sympathy, saying along with Lily that "we're all to blame, really, you can't blame an individual animal for the farm's problems, especially a young'un." And this wide difference of opinions meant that little was done, either to control those young animals who were getting out of hoof and trotter, or to treat the underlying causes of their behaviour. Even the dogs, whose task it was to keep order on the farm, became reluctant to intervene, for fear of being accused of being either too harsh or too lenient.

Curiously, while almost every kind of animal had shared in some measure in the obesity and lack of exercise, the foxes were largely unaffected. They retained their sleek and feral appearance, just as if they were still living in the wild, beyond the farm's boundaries in the distant and as yet uncultivated woods and fields. They ate well but not too much, and they had bought for themselves a large field where they were often to be seen playing fox-holes and other games that kept them strong and fit.

The young foxes, meanwhile, were kept busy not only with learning, but a whole range of activities designed to improve mind and body. By and large, therefore, they kept out of trouble, although there was a tendency for some of the most intelligent to eat too many of the hallucinogenic mushrooms they occasionally bought from the weasels who ran in the surrounding lands, and which commanded astronomical prices.

The New Treadmills

To help relieve the stress of the additional work that the animals were doing, and to burn off some of the fat they had accumulated, many of the ordinary animals considered that they should go to the fields to run, or else sit under a tree and watch the sunset, or pick some wild flowers.

The trouble was, that so much of the land had now been bought and built on and fenced off to make more "efficient" use of it. There was now little space to run in any longer, while the once open vistas of fields had given way to endless dreary obstructions. Only the foxes and the pigs, with their large acreages, continued to enjoy fine views and opportunities for running free.

All was not lost, however, and the entrepreneurial spirit of the animals once again came to the fore. Some of the animals had made photographs of the farm before the great changes that led to so much efficiency and prosperity, and they now began to frame and sell them.

Animals would take their favourites back to their little homes and hang them on the wall to admire. Lily particularly enjoyed pictures of old chicken coops, like the ones which had been knocked down to make way for the factory, shaded by trees and evoking a sense of bucolic ease among the chickens pictured there. Erroll, by contrast, favoured scenes of the American West, with its vast open spaces and herds of buffalo wandering free.

In many ways, some opined, it was more reliable than the old practice of wandering up and down in the fields, since the pictures were always the same, never spoiled by the driving rain or oppressive heat of summer.

"Besides," as Blink remarked one day to Bristle, over a bottle of the most excellent French brandy, at a famous eating hut called the Fat Goose At Play, "your animals can now buy pictures of anything: fields from other farms, exotic fruits and grains and vegetables, beaches with palm trees, snow-capped mountains. This is enriching their lives beyond measure, allowing them the freedom to roam the world from the comfort of their stalls and barns. Breaking them away from the mental monotony of only knowing their own fields and hedgerows. It's about freedom of choice, the freedom that allows an animal to enjoy any scene they want, at any time of the day or night."

Nor was it long before the problem of lack of exercise was solved, after a fashion. Merlin had had a brainwave. Worried himself about the effect of a reduction in physical labour on his own body, he had bought some old treadmills from the pigs and had cleaned and polished one of them, and set it up on a small piece of land he had acquired in the centre of the farm. Every morning, he would exercise by walking round and round the treadmill and after several weeks he became noticeably firmer in tone and his coat glossier than before.

It was not long before other animals were asking to be allowed to share his treadmill. So he fixed all those he had and for a suitable sum, he would let the animals use the treadmills for up to an hour each time. With the dominos he earned, he built shelters over them, so rain or shine, snow or sleet, the animals could exercise to their hearts' content.

The animals were delighted to rediscover the joy of walking and running long distances and found the arrangement highly convenient. They were only too glad to pay. Merlin even did his old friend Erroll a favour. He appointed him the "head instructor" in charge of a group of young stallions whose job it was to help the animals who attended. For a considerable additional sum, some of the more ambitious but less disciplined animals were able to have Erroll or one of his horses stand by their treadmill and hit their buttocks with a switch of willow as they were running round to make sure they did not slacken. So once again, what once had been a symbol of human oppression had been transformed into a symbol of the increasing freedoms the animals of Market Farm enjoyed.

The Cabbage Tournays

Far more popular than the treadmills were the Cabbage Tournays. The treadmills were clearly not just about health, but showed a subconscious desire on the part of the animals to return to the days when physical effort had been part of their everyday lives, and which had now in many cases been replaced by paper shuffling and shopkeeping and various "artistic" trades, such as turnip carving. For the lazier animals, as well as for others, this desire could be fed by watching far more energetic displays by their fellow creatures.

The tournays had started out as fairly informal affairs, in which competing teams of animals would kick a large cabbage around a field, trying to send it through a gap between two trees at either end, an occurrence that was called a "cabbage". Whichever team had notched up the most "cabbages" by the time the vegetable fell apart was adjudged the winner. Erroll, now that he was back in shape, became an enthusiastic player, and even Merlin joined in, though Lily could never be persuaded to put her feathers at risk of mud or sweat or damage.

So popular were the Cabbage Tournays, however, that it was inevitable that the Invisible Snout would work its magic, and bring them into the games of dominos that the foxes never tired of playing. Instead of simple games played after work by a few animals who were particularly interested or talented, animals were organised into teams by the foxes, who paid them to display their skills at a specially cordoned-off field, with animals paying considerable sums of dominos to watch.

These highly athletic animals – the young stallions and heifers were especially impressive – made the cabbage do things with their hoofs that no other animal could hope to achieve, and of course they could run, at least for short distances, at incredible speed. The animals were thrilled by these displays, which made them forget how hard they worked, and how their dominos never seemed to be quite enough to make life truly comfortable. They mooed and clucked and quacked and baaed with delight, and factions would form, some supporting one team and some another. Erroll would go as often as he could, bellowing along with the crowd and waving a brightly coloured blue faction scarf tied to the end of his tail.

More and more tournays were organised, and the events themselves, as well as the results, soon consumed more than half of the time of the entertainers and puppeteers, who responded to the desire of the animals to experience again and again the thrill of the cabbage hurtling between the trees. They and many of the stallkeepers began to pay enormous sums of dominos to have the name of their particular rag or puppet show or stall branded onto the steers or horses playing, in an attempt to attract more trade. The steers and stallions, meanwhile, began to be traded at exorbitant prices, much as such prize animals had been at the agricultural shows in the days when human beings ran the farm.

Not even the fights that accompanied the matches could put the animals off. Despite the constant trading of participants, the animals for some reason identified fiercely with one team or another, and would wave flags with the team brand during games, and sing little songs of encouragement. So strong was the loyalty and identification with what went on upon the field, that they would quickly attack animals supporting the other side, and not even the dogs could always keep control.

So it seemed that while the Invisible Snout was the cult of the foxes, and perhaps even of the pigs, it was the Cabbage Tournays that were the much more manifest religion of the general animal herd, providing clarity, meaning and even transcendence in an otherwise contradictory existence. The animals who could not afford the time or dominos to attend the actual tournays would spend hours watching their re-creation in the puppet shows, a privilege for which they paid anyway.

All of which led, of course, only to an increase in the Great Fattening, as time that might have been spent running around or otherwise in motion, was instead spent standing still, and more often than not, eating.

The Freedom Tree is Pruned

The pigs on the Farm Council were having an ever harder time making good on their promise of "freedom and prosperity for all", the rallying cry that animated, in slightly different variation, all of their speeches. As more and more animals found themselves unable to share in the prosperity that was so vigorously on display, the pigs had to step in with hand-outs of turnips, carrots, corn and the like, known as the Common Trough. Usefully enough, this ever expanding process of doling out vegetables to all and sundry also employed many animals who might otherwise have been idle and the cause of trouble.

It had become, however, enormously costly. In fact, the Common Trough had steadily grown in size and complexity over the years to the point where it seemed that it now involved half the farm, with a quarter of the animals receiving the turnips and a quarter giving them out in enormously intricate and time-consuming rituals. This meant that each year, the

Annual Tithe had to be increased, and the animals who paid the tithe were becoming increasingly resentful. The pigs began to fear that trouble might ensue.

"Easy though the animals are to herd, given their sociable nature and the need to protect their young, if sufficiently roused, there could still be a stampede!" Bristle warned Scratcher at a dinner of Italian white truffles in the Farm House.

The pigs, who had long since given up trying to cover the cost of the Common Trough from the actual tithes collected each year, had naturally turned to borrowing dominos as well, writing ever more of the always popular T-Barns. But the pigs were finding that the more of these IOUs they gave out, the less they were wanted and the more dominos they had to offer in repayment. The truth was that the foxes were becoming a bit fed up with the T-Barns. With all the animals now borrowing willy-nilly, the foxes had plenty of chances to earn more from their own IOUs, which they were giving out right, left and centre to the chickens and sheep and cattle, as well as trading amongst themselves.

Yet the foxes once again came to the rescue of Market Farm, with another very bright idea.

"What you've got to consider, my dear pigs, is to make more of those things on the farm that are still held in common. Use them as a lever to make more of them. Farm activity – that is to say all of farm life – you have to see as a millstone. The more grist is added to the mill, the better it will turn, and the better it turns, the more it can grind, and the better it can grind, the more for everyone," Blink argued, with impeccable logic.

"So what do you mean precisely?" asked Bristle, who was never one to deal in abstractions, but liked the smell of action and energy. "How are we going to add more grist, as you call it?"

"What we need to do," Blink advised, narrowing his eyes to a sharp focus, "is to give the animals a direct share of ownership in the common properties."

The pigs, Bristle included, did not quite like the sound of this, but they realised that the tithes were no longer enough for them to be able to make good on the promises they had made. And the idea of asking for more in tithes would surely be very unpopular, and none of the pigs were brave enough to propose it.

"But will it work? Will the animals be interested?"

"Of course. It all depends how you present the idea. And it all depends what you present as the idea, especially the first time."

"The first time?"

"Yes, once you've done it once, you'll be amazed how good it feels," said Blink, smiling so that his teeth shone in the light from the window. "All we need to do is to start with something big. Something that every animal knows and trusts. Something that if just one animal has a piece of, every single other animal will want a piece of."

So it was that the spring of one particular year saw one of the greatest and most controversial initiatives that had ever occurred at Market Farm, even after all the things that had happened since the foxes began to transform it. One day, the pigs announced that they had decided to sell the Freedom Tree.

The animals were shocked.

"The Freedom Tree is the very symbol of all we've achieved and all that Market Farm stands for!" shouted Merlin, in a rare display of emotion. "It was meant to stand forever, a sacred part of the farm that truly belongs to each and every one of us!"

Most of the animals felt the same way. But the pigs went out of their way to promote the idea, through interviews that had been carefully scripted by some of the rabbits, whose sensitive little pink noses were ideal for sniffing the sentiments of the animals.

"It is a logical evolution of everything we have been doing," Scratcher explained, managing in true pig fashion to tell the truth while lying at the same time. "Selling the Freedom Tree means that each one of us has a chance to buy their very own part of the tree, and thereby to benefit from the blessing offered by the magnificent oak in a direct and personal way, as it suits them. As it now stands, it is no more than a vague, collective representation of freedom. What we are proposing is that each animal will own a tangible portion of freedom in his or her own right."

"Furthermore, the money raised will be put towards collective good causes, such as supervised play pens for the younger animals, who are now left alone more often than they should be, and more turnips for the Common Trough."

"And in any case, not all of the tree will be sold off. The most substantial part of it will be left standing where it is, to preserve our heritage, safe under your pigs' trotters."

There was much lowing and clucking and bleating, and for a whole week, fierce debates raged among the animals, many of whom felt that holding something sacred and in common was a bond without which the farm would have no real existence. Yet in the end, the sale of the tree could not be stopped.

The foxes, whose idea it had been, kindly arranged, in exchange for a not inconsiderable "fee", to conduct the sale. They were even generous enough to agree to buy most of the tree in case the animals were not sufficiently enthusiastic. They offered commissions to persuade their fellow animals to buy. How hard these fortunate ones worked!

Their arguments were also crafted by the rabbits, working together with the foxes this time, and while the pigs had expressed lofty sentiments clearly designed to appeal to the animals' finer natures, they addressed rather different instincts.

Lily had never bought anything other than fineries, feeling she did not understand all this buying and selling of sheds and stalls, and had never managed to amass enough dominos to participate. But her interest was finally piqued by the Freedom Tree.

"Think of the rarity of the pieces of oak to be sold off," said the goat who came to explain the concept to her. "This would ensure that their value would only increase as time went on, and great riches will await those who buy early and in quantity."

Nor was Lily the only one to buy. How persuasive were the tales of the wealth to be made "down the line" by selling parts in the tree to those who had been unfortunate enough to get none. What a benefit the slivers of wood would be to the animals and their offspring!

So successful were the exhortations that as the sale day approached, interest had reached fever pitch and most of the animals were more than eager to buy. A great crowd assembled to see the foxes at work as they attacked the Freedom Tree eagerly with chain saws. One by one, under the whirring blades, the great oak's branches came crashing down, splintering as they fell. When only the trunk was left, they set to work slicing the branches into small rounds of wood. It was a work of shock and awe, that left the animals with an apprehensive excitement.

Most were therefore disappointed to receive only a small number of wood rounds that seemed to bear almost no relation to the once magnificent tree. The bulk had gone to the foxes.

Fortunately, these worthy animals were generous enough to sell on the rounds that they had bought – admittedly at higher prices – so by the end, nearly all the animals of the farm had enough to make them happy. They proudly took them home to their families, boasting how many they had bought and secretly waiting for the day when some luckless chicken would pay a pig's ransom for their holding.

The success of the sale of the Freedom Tree emboldened the foxes and the pigs to even greater efforts to foster the well being of the farm by selling off even more of the common land. One by one, the fields and barns and granaries were disposed of. This allowed the pigs to make ever more extravagant promises of "prosperity for all" – the latest and most succinct statement of their guiding philosophy – and to make good on these with more gifts of grain or turnips to those who needed or clamoured for them. There would be no limits to the pigs' ability to increase the Common Trough!

The trouble was, that the longer this went on, the more the animals began to see this dole as the natural order of things, and to regard the Farm Council as existing to provide abundance for every animal. The foxes sometimes warned sternly that it was immoral for the Council to give out the farm's wealth in this way, and no good would come of it. This kind of charity was something they themselves would never ask for, since it would offend the Invisible Snout! But so handsome were the rewards of their involvement in the sales of the common land, that their opposition was always half-hearted. Indeed, as the sales went on, the foxes were very quickly able to replace their straw huts with much sturdier and more comfortable wooden sheds.

Lily clung on to her shaving, keeping it safe but taking it out to admire it every now and again, and almost willing it to "do well". Erroll had borrowed some dominos to buy more, and was overjoyed to be able to sell on some of them at a fine profit, as he had always known would be the case. Once again, Merlin proved the odd animal out. However much Lily and Erroll, let alone the goats or rabbits, tried to persuade him, he would not be moved.

"It's a travesty," he said, "and no good will come of it."

The Great Paperchase

While the free turnips and grain were a great help, as prices of land and barns continued to rise, many of the less able or less fortunate chickens and sheep who had been left out of the great speculation in land entirely, began angrily complaining about the unfairness of the situation to the rag writers and the puppeteers. Nor were these reticent in their criticism of the pigs and in blaming them for the state of affairs and failing to provide "prosperity for all".

The pigs knew that their rule of the farm rested on their ability to convince animals that they had made their pledge of "prosperity for all" in good faith. If ever it were suspected that instead, the farm was about "prosperity for some", let alone "prosperity for all pigs and foxes", disorder would ensue, "as sure as eggs is eggs".

But how to make sure that every animal could buy a shed, with prices soaring so high, and with the foxes unwilling to lend out dominos to animals they suspected had no hope of returning them? The answer was for the pigs to set up a shed of their own and to lend as freely as they liked to any animal in need. So this is what was done. It was understandably popular, and flocks of chickens and sheep rushed to the hut to collect their dominos, which they used to buy whatever little fold or shed was still available.

One might have expected the foxes to be concerned, and in a way they were, for if matters continued in this way, soon every animal would sign IOUs with the pigs, which would make it impossible for them to keep doubling their dominos. The whole scheme which they had laboured so hard to create would come crashing down and with it, the prosperity that was their birthright.

But the resourcefulness of the foxes was ever at hand to bring new marvels to Market Farm. Blink hit upon the idea of creating dominos not based on the now almost forgotten nose rings, but in relation to dominos that were already in circulation.

"In this way," he argued to the pigs, "the power of freedom will become greatly magnified and will allow us to lend even the least likely looking chicken even more dominos than she needs to buy a coop. After all, the prices of land and barns will always increase and at some point will be worth double the original IOU. There is nothing to lose!"

Blink also reasoned that it would be much less risky if the IOUs for the dominos were cut into little pieces, shuffled up and auctioned off, rather than being held by the fox who had lent the dominos in the first place. "The more widely the IOUs are shared out the better," he continued, "and the less that any animal knows about the real thing the IOU represents, the better also. They will exist in their own pure form."

At a private meeting with the understandably nervous

rabbits, Blink and the other foxes prevailed on the Chief Rabbit to assent to this dramatic innovation and before long, the foxes were engaged in a healthy exchange of these snippets of paper. So greatly did they benefit from this activity, that even the wooden houses they had erected were torn down and replaced by magnificent edifices of brick, almost rivalling that of the Farm House itself! These sturdy buildings were useful not only for protecting all of the paper that the foxes had produced from the rain and the ants, but were a potent symbol for the pigs and other animals of just how solid were the foundations of Market Farm's new era of prosperity.

In fact, Market Farm was now producing so much paper that even these brick houses were not enough. Whole barns had to be turned over to storing it. Since the paper was clearly much more valuable than anything else – indeed, it defined the very social order of the farm – farm equipment and sometimes even farm produce was in some cases turfed out of the barns to make way for it.

So great were the fortunes to be made in trading land and erecting barns that it became pretty well the only thing that the animals were interested in. After all, any animal who stuck to his time worn furrow, or was silly enough to spend his time merely growing food, was soon unable to afford anything very much. From swapping the land, to building the barns, to buying and selling barns both built and un-built and planned and half planned, more and more animals had jumped on the barn-building boom. This made the foxes ever happier, as the merry-go-round of the dominos spun faster and faster.

Slowly but surely, therefore, the productive fields of the farm shrank until they extended to a mere half of their former size, though curiously, very few animals remarked upon this. After all, with prices rising just as the foxes had predicted, it did not matter that the amount they earned from working remained the same. All they had to do was to sign another IOU, based on the higher value of their shed or chicken coop, and they could live better than ever before. It was like magic!

By contrast, the pigs, while pleased with the general frenzy of activity among the increasingly desperate animals, were becoming a little alarmed at the volume of paper. Yet according to the foxes, the problem was not too much paper, but too little! They explained that the entire system would eventually run out of steam unless another radical improvement was made. The resourcefulness of the foxes was far from exhausted. It was necessary, they argued, for them to be able not just to lend dominos and trade IOUs, but to lend dominos they did not have and hence to buy dominos from animals who did not own any either. It would, said the foxes, make them much more ready to keep buying and selling, thus providing the farm with even more of the hope and trust in the future that had made every animal so hard working.

The pigs had a hard time understanding how the lending of dominos that did not exist might benefit the farm, or how more crops might be grown or eggs laid as a result. Yet they had to admit that the foxes had tended to be right so far, and that indeed the animals were now working morning and night to the point of exhaustion, so that production must be increasing. So they gave the foxes the benefit of the doubt.

Yet although the pigs noticed that as a result prices seemed to rise even more precipitously than before, overall, just as the foxes had predicted, it made the merry-go-round of the trade in dominos even livelier. And since the pigs, for the benefit of the farm, exacted a toll each time dominos changed hands, they were well content to let things run. Besides, the Chief Rabbit, chewing calmly on a carrot, assured them that the more dominos were exchanged, the better for all concerned. "If some foxes want to borrow dominos from other foxes who don't have them, then that is entirely the foxes' affair," he reasoned.

Mountains and Molehills

Of course, even the stupidest of the animals suspected that it was quite likely that the magic of transforming a real object, such as a parcel of land or a milking shed, into a piece of paper, would not necessarily work in reverse on every occasion. Already, there had been cases where an animal had not paid back an IOU, which had led to lengthy and often noisy arguments. So far, such cases had been very rare, such was the hard work and dedication of the animals in their labours. But as the stock of paper grew ever larger in relation to the things on the farm, concern steadily grew. "By the Almighty Boar, if all these papers were ever to be returned, we'd need ten or more Market Farms to pay it back," said one of the farm's more sceptical donkeys.

The pigs themselves were becoming increasingly worried. The foxes, however, reassured them.

"Look, the plain fact is that the vast majority of dominos now in barns around the farm bear no relation to any real things, not even to nose rings." Blink explained in his measured but forceful tones, to Bluffer, Scratcher and Bristle, who for once had put aside their admittedly minor differences to "seek some clarity on the issue". "They are just dominos that relate to other dominos. So in fact everything is cancelled out and this means it's all perfectly safe, since in fact, nothing exists."

Quite why the majority of dominos were dedicated to no discernible real purpose or why this was "safer" was beyond the reasoning of not just Bluffer, Scratcher and Bristle, but any of the pigs. But once again they were forced to agree that it had all worked so far, and that activity among the animals on the farm was becoming ever more frenzied, which just made their own lives all the more comfortable, as it increased the tithes they collected.

The foxes did concede, however, that the likelihood of an animal not paying back their IOU was becoming ever more difficult to judge, given the veritable mountains of paper now on the farm, and the huge variety of things both real and imaginary it was supposed to represent. They therefore proposed that each IOU would benefit from a system that would enhance the safeguards already in place with the rabbits.

"What is needed is for an animal quite unconnected with the others, who would be able to assess each IOU and tell the animals how safe it is – a sort of canary in the coalmine," Blink proposed. "Although the job would have to be made more attractive, of course," he added, with a typically fox-like sense of humour.

And so it was that the moles finally came into their own. Their eyesight was so poor that they could barely read what was written on the IOUs, and admittedly they spent most of their lives deep underground. But it was reasoned that this was a guarantee of their independence. Furthermore, the rabbits maintained that the moles' exceptionally keen sense of smell and their ability to detect the minutest of vibrations, made them ideal guardians of probity as far as the IOUs were concerned.

So the pigs and foxes now submitted all of their IOUs to the moles. The moles sniffed each very carefully, before shooting down into their holes for several days of quiet contemplation. Then they would pop up again, and ink a number of paw marks onto the paper. Those with three paw marks – or "triple paws" as they became known – were considered the most worthy, and would sell for the highest prices.

Even the snippets of IOUs were graded in this way. A fox would take the snippets, shuffle them like a deck of cards and give the deck to a mole, who would automatically affix three paw marks to the top papers, two to the papers lower down and so on.

And, *mirabile dictu*, since the moles were paid for their sniffing by the foxes, the entire check and balance that contributed so much to the safety of the farm would cost the ordinary farm animals nothing at all!

A Taste of Prosperity

Despite the problems of muck and fat, and the stubborn resistance of a strangely growing number of the animals to make the most of the opportunities to "better themselves" as the foxes called it, an air of shiny prosperity pervaded the farm.

The three friends were also content, each in their own way. Merlin's treadmills and his shop were bringing him a steady flow of dominos, which he was careful to turn into nose rings as and when he could. He too had acquired a rather larger stall in a quiet part of the farm. Much to the astonishment of his friends, he had bought it without writing any IOUs to the foxes.

"You must be mad, Merlin!" Erroll told him one day as they were enjoying a refreshing drink of barley wine. "The foxes are practically giving dominos away. It's almost a crime not to borrow them."

Merlin was not to be moved, however. "I'm a magician, after all. My job is to turn paper into brass," he joked, and something almost resembling a smile flickered across his lips.

Even more astonished were the friends when he invited them for dinner. Although still rather small, the stall was exquisitely fitted out with fine oak floors, paintings on the walls of abstract animals, and comfortable furniture. They dined off fine china using silver cutlery of the latest design, eating the most exquisite delicacies and some fine elderflower wine.

"Merlin you're a marvel," said Lily, ruffling her now blue tinted feathers. "You never cease to amaze me. And there I was, thinking that you were some kind of monk, and never interested in all these luxuries. What a fantastic little home you've made."

Even Merlin could not suppress a touch of pride in his achievement. Yet Merlin's new dwelling paled in comparison to that which Erroll had moved into. Being a larger animal – "in both size and in spirit" he liked to joke – it was an altogether roomier, newly-built barn with a vast living room and dining room full of comfortable furniture. Here he entertained his friends in grand style, with lashings of his favourite foods and mugs of barley wine.

Lily was goggle-eyed at it all, and cluck-clucked her way around in amazement, her earrings and necklaces jingling as she went. "Why, you're living like a pig!" she exclaimed, offering him the highest praise that a farm animal could give.

"It's not the only one, Lily," Erroll explained. "I have three other sheds of different sizes that are all rented out."

"But how could you ever save so many dominos?" Lily asked incredulously.

"That's your trouble," Erroll replied. "It's not about saving dominos, it's the opposite, despite what Merlin says. It's about how many you can borrow. Saving dominos is for the birds –

well, you know what I mean. I borrow and I buy a shed, and when it goes up, I borrow some more on it and buy another shed. And so on. In a few years' time I want to have not just sheds but barns. Then you'll really see how I can live!"

Erroll's enthusiasm could not be contained, and he brought more mugs of barely wine for his friends. Merlin nursed his drink thoughtfully, while Lily's head was spinning.

Why was she always so stupid and timid and unable to make up her mind, always running around like a two-headed chicken? Yes, perhaps she was silly to spend so many of the dominos she had worked so hard for on feather-tints and the like. She made up her mind, she would finally follow the lead of Erroll and those like him and buy a little coop all of her own.

So the very next day, she scraped together all the dominos she had and did just that. It was a small coop and suffered somewhat from being a little too close to the waste pits, which for all of the pigs' efforts had only got larger. But it was home, and it was hers. And Fat-tail, the kindly old fox who lent her the dominos had given her enough to buy not just the coop itself, but some modest furnishings for it. It was truly heaven on earth!

The Chickens Come Home to Roost

Not long after one Harvest Festival, where the size of the Harvest Pie seemed only to confirm that an unbounded era of prosperity stretched ahead for the animals of Market Farm, some of the foxes who had built up sizeable plots of farmland and groups of buildings over the years, began to sell. They generally found more than willing buyers among the other animals, who like Erroll were by now accustomed to think of the buying of land and buildings as a sure way to enjoy the riches of farm life while escaping the daily grind of work – indeed the only way.

Indeed Erroll too was just waiting for an opportunity to "buy on the dip" as he termed it, hoping that a suitable barn would come his way. Merlin, by contrast, seemed even more concerned to convert his dominos into nose rings, and had even decided to sell one little shed he had bought to rent out.

Thanks to the tremendous cleverness of the foxes, of course, it had also become ever easier for the "ordinary" animals (for such they had now come to regard themselves) to pay the by now huge sums needed to buy even the smallest plot of land or most insignificant hut. Curiously, the more unaffordable the land and buildings became, the more the animals – the animals apart from the foxes that is – became convinced that they were worth buying. It was not only Lily who had offered to pledge her entire life savings in order to gain, as it was called, "a rung on the ladder", some had pledged those of their children to gain such freedom. Never before in the history of Market Farm had there been such abundance, nor such freedom to pursue the accumulation of riches. How proud the Snout must be of its creatures!

But the euphoria was not to last. No one could quite remember how it happened or when it happened or who noticed it first, but as the frenzy of the trading in IOUs went ever higher, one day, out of the blue – or perhaps it was from the mouth of a kid or suckling pig – a rumour was heard that one of the foxes had been unable to make good on his promises to another fox.

Fang, the fox in question, was not well liked, being an ugly, aggressive and ill-mannered sort of animal. He relied entirely on borrowing dominos from one fox one day to pay another fox the next day, and his luck had finally run out. He had now been reduced to the position where he had to use some of his stock of nose rings. Not entirely to the rabbits' surprise, however, it was discovered that far from the amount he should have had, Fang's nose rings amounted to only one hundredth part of the amount of dominos he owed. As soon as the other foxes heard of this, there was panic, and they stampeded to his house, hoping to be the first to the nose-ring box.

Fang ran to the pigs for help, thinking that some of the nose rings stored in the great Central Piggy Bank in case of emergency might be drawn upon. But the pigs had never really liked him either, and told him there was nothing they could do. "The rot has to stop somewhere," Bluffer said to his fellow pigs, "and letting Fang get what's coming will help restore confidence." In a matter of minutes, Fang's piggy bank was smashed and emptied, and all he could do was to run around the farmyard howling.

The alarm felt by the pigs and foxes did not abate, however; quite the opposite. The other animals had heard of Fang's difficulties, and there were reports that some had gone to collect dominos from the foxes, just in case. In short, there was a danger that the desire to turn paper back into nose rings would ripple across the entire farm. The rabbits suspected (for even they did not really have any idea) that not one fiftieth the required number of nose rings could be found if needed.

An urgent meeting was held with the Chief Rabbit and his fellow rabbits. After some time, the rabbits and pigs, led by Bluffer and the Chief Rabbit, assembled to ask the rag writers and puppeteers to transmit an important message to the farm.

"The pigs in charge of the Tithe Barn and the Chief Rabbit at the Farm Forge are working to sort out the difficulty concerning the nose rings. It is purely temporary, it affects only one of the foxes, and no other animal is involved. So there is no need for concern. All will continue as before. All animals may rest sound in their stalls, their coops and their meadows," Bluffer solemnly intoned.

The animals, who by now had heard the shocking news that a fox had been caught out, were reassured. Despite the odd bleat and cluck, they went back to their homes, in any case weary after the long hours of worry and with the humdrum tasks of their lives to face, such as feeding their young and preparing for the next long (and seemingly ever longer) working day.

Merlin was very agitated, however, and ran to his friend Lily. He caught her at a late supper, relaxing after a hard day at the factory, where she now worked long hours to find the dominos she needed to pay the IOU.

"Lily, you must sell this coop before it's too late!" he told her.

"What do you mean, too late? There's nothing to worry about. It's just a mess up between the foxes. Bluffer said so, I saw it on the puppet show. You're worrying over nothing, Merlin," she said calmly, although as usual, she was not sure which side of the argument was right. "In any case, I've worked so hard for this little place, and I won't part with it."

It pained Merlin to be unable to persuade Lily, but he was even less successful with Erroll.

"Don't be an ass Merlin!" explained Erroll, rather incautiously. "This is the time to buy, not sell! Buy low, sell high, that's the big brass rule! If I had the dominos I'd buy now. After all, what comes down always goes up!"

Yet while most ordinary animals were convinced that it would be "farming as usual", a noticeable air of tension had crept in among the foxes and pigs. Like Merlin, many of the foxes now began to cash in some of their dominos for nose rings and to call in as many IOUs as they could. All of the foxes, who had once laughed and joked with each other as the animals queued up to deposit dominos or sign new IOUs, now looked at each other suspiciously. Many of the smartest looking foxes with the shiniest coats had also relied almost entirely on swapping dominos and IOUs with other foxes, and had little connection with the dull round of exchanges with the other farm animals that the larger and slower foxes like Fat-tail had conducted. These foxes, as the potential problem in the trade in IOUs emerged, came most under the cloud of suspicion.

It was not long before the foxes became reluctant to swap IOUs with each other at all and sought to preserve as big a stash of nose rings as each could muster. Suddenly, even the most creditworthy chicken or cow suddenly found it hard to obtain the by now huge sums needed to pay for the land and buildings they desired.

In a matter of days, optimism turned to pessimism. Once the herds of cattle and flocks of sheep, geese, ducks and chickens had all convinced each other that the buying of land and farm-buildings was the only and sure path to salvation, as the prices would always go up. They were now in equally full agreement that the reverse was likely to be the case. Everyone wanted to sell and no one wanted to buy. This at least had the virtue of keeping prices stable, but it was only a matter of time before the dam holding back the tide of downward expectation burst. First, a pig sold a barn for just a few dominos less than she had wanted. Then a young boar cut the price of a stall he didn't in any case use. Before long, sheep, cows and chickens were all selling for much less than they had once asked.

Even Erroll quickly sold one of his sheds, but soon found he could not sell more. Within weeks, it seemed, most of the great wealth he thought he had accumulated, had indeed evaporated. Most of the dominos he had taken out of the sheds he had bought would have to be put back in again somehow, so little were these buildings now in demand.

Lily just didn't know what to do or who to believe, but was more than shocked to discover that a coop just like the one she had bought had sold for a good deal less than she had paid for it. The poor chicken wept bitter tears at the thought.

Yet this was just the beginning of what later was called

the "Great Winnowing". Sheep who had recently bought milking stalls with dominos borrowed from the foxes on the expectation that they too, finally, would be able to make a quick and handsome sale, found themselves unable to make good on the IOUs.

In many cases, they would have simply abandoned the useless buildings, and given them back to the foxes. However, the milking stalls were of no use to the foxes, who would have been unable to sell them on, since there were too many milking stalls already on the farm. Animals who tried this found that the once smooth and friendly foxes reverted very much to type, and their smiles of welcome quickly became snarls of warning.

As Blink explained at a rather fraught meeting with the much disconcerted Bluffer, the IOUs could not be reneged upon.

"The sanctity of the IOU is at the very heart of the workings of the Invisible Snout," he maintained. "What is written is written, and cannot be unwritten. All our freedoms would turn to dust."

The Great Winnowing

It was not long, however, before outright panic began to set in. And ironically, it was among the foxes themselves that it set in first. For all their cleverness, the entire edifice built of dominos and IOUs was so complex and so unstable that even they could no longer tell what anything was worth. The more they became convinced that a fellow fox would not be able to come up with the nose rings, the more quickly they tried to grab them from him.

The other farm animals were secretly delighted at the sight of foxes sharing the pain and bewilderment which they had felt so often in the past. Yet their pleasure at the sight of their plight was tempered with a tinge of fear. If a fox could get into such difficulties, what chance did they have if things got really out of hoof?

They were right to be concerned. Fang's trail of dominos led straight to the door of Fat-tail, proprietor of the largest of all the foxes' counting houses, thanks to his affable and carefree nature. For unlike Fang, Fat-tail had been a great friend to all animals, such as Lily, and had both kept their dominos safe and lent out huge amounts of dominos to those animals often shunned by the other foxes. The hitherto unappreciated inter-connectedness of the whole system meant that Fat-tail too was in trouble, as the other foxes fought like wolves to grab his nose rings, with fur flying.

Like the bursting of a great storm cloud, the truth dawned that in fact few of the foxes had the ability to meet their obligation to turn their dominos back into nose rings, and that many of the animals would not be able to repay their IOUs, foxes included, however sacred they were. With the most incredible speed, the Great Winnowing had begun.

Soon, more and more foxes were rumoured to be in trouble and any fox who had nose rings left, held them tightly in his box, refusing to lend any more dominos or trade any more IOUs with absolutely anyone, since no animal could any longer be trusted. It seemed that even an IOU that was "triple paws", was simply not worth what it should have been, perhaps no more than the paper itself! Fear gripped the farm as never before.

"Oh whatever will I do!" clucked Lily, flapping her wings wildly. "All the nose rings I have are at Fat-tail's counting house, and I shan't be able to get any of them back!"

Nor was Erroll any less concerned, for he too had deposited his nose rings with Fat-tail, and for once, his abundant energy turned not to optimism, but outrage. He ran about the farmyard bellowing loudly at the top of his lungs that the pigs and the foxes together should be made to pay for bringing the farm to such a state of collapse.

Wholesale panic was only minutes away, and the pigs asked the foxes what to do. After taking the foxes' advice, they trotted briskly along to the Forge and together with the Chief Rabbit, they all went as quickly as ever they had in their lives to the entertainers. Bluffer made a portentous announcement.

"Fellow animals," he said. "Fat-tail must be in a position to fulfil his obligations. Indeed all foxes must be in a position to fulfil their obligations. So the wealth of the Central Piggy Bank will be used to guarantee all of their dominos. You have nothing to fear, and you can carry on as normal."

For a short time, there was great relief. The thought of the pigs, who collected all the tithes, making sure that everything would be all right was more than reassuring to the animals of Market Farm.

The trouble was, whatever the pigs promised, no one was sure how it would work. The foxes in particular continued to hold tight onto the tails of their piggy banks. Nor was it long before the Great Winnowing that began with the dominos started to affect daily life. No animal was sure any longer what to do. Fields were left unsown, and rows of vegetables unweeded, crops were not planted, for no animal knew whether they could be sold. It was as if the tremendous energy that had for a time made Market Farm active beyond the dreams of any horse or cow, and had enriched the pigs and foxes in particular beyond even their wildest imaginings, was now pulling everything down. What the paper had wrought, it would destroy.

The foxes called a secret meeting with the Inner Council to discuss the matter. The pigs were frightened and angry, and some even had the audacity to suggest that it must be the foxes themselves who should sort out the mess, and use some of the wealth they had amassed over the years to make sure that confidence was restored. Surely, they could add some nose rings from their great personal hoards in Vegetarian Villas to

121

the boxes in the houses.

The foxes resisted this fiercely. As Blink, according to his mirror still the sleekest of all, explained in careful tones, "Taking such an immoral step as you are advocating would send the entire system we have built with such love and care, and which has created so much prosperity, into the abyss! What we're doing is the Snout's work. It is only through our work that the farm can prosper. Indeed, without it, there would be no activity on the farm at all. It is not for our own benefit as foxes that we have made our proposals, but for the benefit of all the animals on Market Farm! The flow of dominos and IOUs must continue, for our sake and for the good of all the farm!"

The pigs, however, were at a loss. They did not understand exactly what could be done, but they knew that above all, confidence had to be restored among the animals, who might otherwise even hold the pigs responsible for not protecting the farm from the foxes. This, after all, had once been their task in life and one of the reasons the other animals accepted their rule!

The moles attempted to help by taking a second sniff at the dominos, scratching out some of the marks they had made so much sense of only some months before. But to no avail. The foxes were now relying mainly on their own noses to decide what an IOU was worth, and the answer in most cases was "not enough".

In the end, therefore, the pigs were prepared to agree to whatever solution the foxes proposed. The only IOUs that any animal had any confidence in any more were those of the pigs, the T-Barns backed by the nose rings that every animal knew (or thought they knew) were safely stored up in the great Central Piggy Bank.

So the pigs would ask the Chief Rabbit to give T-Barns to the foxes in exchange for the foxes' own IOUs, however worthless these latter were. What was more, the Chief Rabbit would be asked to print as many dominos as needed and lend them to the foxes in return for even more IOUs from the foxes.

It was a brilliant scheme! At a stroke, the foxes' problem had been resolved. As a result, said the foxes, the basic freedoms that were at the heart of Market Farm, were preserved. At the same time all the animals, great and small, could rest assured that all was well and that their dominos were as good as brass. What is more, the foxes would have something to keep them occupied, as they would be the ones arranging the complex business of swapping round the T-Barns and IOUs on behalf of the farm – for which, of course, they would be paid a sizeable fee, as was only right and proper.

Having made their decision, the foxes and the pigs presented it to the Chief Rabbit and his fellow rabbits.

So Scratcher and Bristle held a meeting with the Chief Rabbit.

"What we need you to do," Scratcher explained, "is to give T-Barns to the foxes in exchange for the foxes' IOUs."

"With respect, your swineship, it could be that the IOUs from the foxes that you are asking me to accept are worthless. While it may work to restore confidence in the foxes in the short run, it could undermine the animals' confidence in the Central Piggy Bank in the longer run," the Rabbit explained, twitching nervously the while.

"Nevertheless, this is what will be done," said Scratcher. What is more, you will print as many dominos as are needed and lend them to the foxes in return for even more IOUs which the foxes will give you."

The Chief Rabbit was not happy with the proposal, since

it seemed to him that the animals most responsible for the looming catastrophe would be precisely those who would benefit most from this attempt to stave it off. He also knew that the Central Piggy Bank could be left stuffed full of a lot of worthless pieces of paper and that, memories being short, he might be blamed if it all went wrong. But looking into the narrowing eyes of the foxes, and taking account of their very sharp teeth, was enough to persuade him that agreement was the only course of action. After all, he was only a rabbit.

The pigs pushed the Chief Rabbit before the assembled crowds of entertainers and puppeteers. Understandably, the rabbit was nervous – first, because he was, after all, a rabbit and hence it was in his very nature; secondly, because the task he faced, that of saving Market Farm, was probably beyond the ability of any animal save the Almighty Boar; and thirdly, because the angry and confused mob of animals had come to regard him as the "iron anvil" that they could depend on. His nose twitched, his pink eyes stared into the middle distance and his feet thumped the ground agitatedly. He cleared his throat striving to sound calm.

"My fellow animals," he quavered. "I can understand that you are worried. But have faith. We have guided you before and we will guide you in the future. I have spent all my life eating carrots and celery, and looking at pieces of paper just like the ones you are worried about. We will be taking every action we can to ensure that there is enough paper to go round, that every fox is a reliable fox and that there is no need to clamour after nose rings. There is nothing to fear but fear itself. Paper is as paper does. All's well that ends well. Amen."

This said, the Chief Rabbit and his fellow rabbits ran off to start up the printing press. Indeed, such was the urgency of the need for nose rings from the foxes, and the quantity required, that the only solution was to smash the Central Piggy Bank, a task the rabbits carried out with great reluctance, and the pigs observed with considerable disquiet.

The foxes, meanwhile, breathed great sighs of relief that their worthless IOUs had been replaced with those from the Central Piggy Bank, so that their own wealth and standing were indeed once again, solid as brass.

"To think that we had come within a whisker of being as poor as the merest chicken! What would that have said about the state of the world!" said Blink.

But above all, the rabbits and the pigs and the foxes all knew that this event must at all costs be kept secret from the other animals in the farm, and so a new Piggy Bank was fashioned straight away, using the shards on the floor of the Tithe Barn. Only this time, the Piggy Bank and its slot were made slightly larger, to accommodate all the paper it was expected to hold.

The Election of Squeaky

It so happened that the Great Winnowing coincided with The Farm Council Elections. This gave the animals some hope that if only the blue pigs could be ousted, the pink pigs would take things in trotter and perhaps teach the foxes a lesson.

Originally, the Council elections had been rather sober affairs, with serious speeches offering sometimes widely differing views of what to do on the farm, especially as regards the extensive common lands, which the animals followed also with some seriousness. However, the great reforms, the general frenzy of activity on the farm, and not least the profusion of puppet shows and entertainment rags, had led to a radical change in the way the elections worked. The animals, it was supposed, needed to be entertained, not bored with tales of grain production and ploughshares, or births and deaths. It was to their sentiments, not their reason, that the ambitious pig must appeal if he were to be chosen to sit in Council.

Election time was thus very exciting for the pigs, as well as for the rag writers and puppeteers, who were never stuck for a good story at this time of year. Weeks ahead of the election day, the pigs who were standing for Council seats would dress up in the appropriate colours and parade around the farm, beaming at every animal they met, shaking their hooves and claws, and hugging any newborns they were lucky enough to chance upon, all the while followed by a gaggle of entertainers. Parties were thrown and speeches delivered containing all sorts of promises made to each and every kind of animal. So confusing was it all that apart from the colours, few animals could tell the two groups apart, so that they tended to choose largely according to whether they liked pink or blue, with little change from year to year. After all, they sensed, the message from both groups each year was essentially the same – "prosperity for all".

The year of the Great Winnowing, the pigs were much more entertaining than usual, and the highlight was a series of mud-slinging contests at which pigs from either group flung mud at each other, with a prize awarded to the pig who made the most mud stick on his or her opponent. There was also a great deal of debate about what to do regarding the foxes, although both groups appeared to favour being very tough on them and punishing them for the mess they had created and which they, the pigs had been forced to clean up.

When she remembered to cast her ballot, Lily always chose the pink pigs, and this year she was especially keen not only because of the frightening mess that the blue pigs had made of things, but also because of the new pink candidate, Squeaky. Squeaky, it was generally agreed, spoke very charmingly, said all the right things and was so very clean that almost no mud stuck to him.

Although Erroll insisted he would always choose the blue pigs come what may, Merlin decided that he too would cast his lot for Squeaky. This was not because he was charmed by his speech as relayed by the puppet shows, but like many of the animals on the farm, he simply thought that a change might be better than no change.

According to this precise logic, the animals over-whelmingly chose the pink pigs, who had been out of favour for most of the time in the recent golden years, and so it was that the leadership of Market Farm passed from Bluffer to Squeaky. The animals watched as Squeaky's first speech on the lawn in front of the Farm House was mimed in all the puppet shows.

"My fellow animals," he cried, smiling confidently and sincerely, picking out with his gaze an individual sheep or goat or horse. "Today I promise you change. I promise you bold action now and more bold action in the future. I promise you a return to the true values of Market Farm. And, of course, I promise you, prosperity for all!" The animals were wildly pleased, and clucked, mooed and baaed with delight!

The Hole Gets Deeper

After the election celebrations, Squeaky had assembled his fellow pigs and given another inspiring speech.

"We must make good on the promises we have made to our fellow animals," he began, his pink skin gleaming from the result of his latest bath. "We are not going to listen to the foxes who had been advising Bluffer. These foxes have exerted an outrageous influence over the Farm Council in recent times. So our first duty to the animals of Market Farm will be to find different foxes, smarter foxes, more reliable foxes, more honest foxes to guide us in our actions. In short, foxes of an entirely different nature who will help ensure that 'prosperity for all' is no empty promise."

And at first, the clever scheme to swap the foxes' IOUs with those of the pigs appeared to have achieved very little. The foxes still hoarded most of their dominos, preferring instead to make hay from the merry-go-round of swapping the IOUs and T-Barns. Altogether, an air of mutual suspicion still lay thick across the fields and farmyard. The ordinary animals were no longer able to borrow the dominos needed to buy and sell as freely as they had done before.

Many animals were desperate to sell things they did not need, since one consequence of the Great Winnowing was that the activity of the farm had wound down considerably, with some animals having no work to do, and others much less. Scratching a living, let alone enjoying carved turnips, was suddenly proving difficult, though somewhat helped by the Common Trough. Whatever Squeaky had promised, the plight of the ordinary animals just seemed to be getting worse and worse.

Lily and Erroll were suffering along with the rest of the animals. Lily was still laying eggs in the factory, as many as she possibly could. But what had looked like a good deal from Fat-tail turned out to be less generous than it seemed, as the amount she needed to return on the IOU steadily increased.

"Oh Erroll," she said, the tears brimming in her little red eyes and running down her cheeks in rivulets of sorrow. "I've had to sell the coop. But it's worth so much less now than when I bought it. In fact, it's worth even less than I owe to Fat-tail. It looks like I'll have to keep working away all my life, and still end up with nothing!"

So it was that Lily sold not only her coop, at a knock-down price, but all the little comforts she had built up over the years, for whatever she could get for them, from whichever crow or rat or mouse would buy them. It was indeed a pitiful sight to see her handing over these mementos of prosperity and hope, in exchange, as it seemed for nothing more than sadness in her eyes and drooping, bedraggled feathers.

Erroll was scarcely in better shape. With so little activity on the farm now, he was unable to earn extra dominos as he had once done, and he was embarrassed to think of asking Merlin for his old job on the treadmills. One by one he had sold off his sheds, some of which were worth more than he had paid for them, making up for those now worth much less. He had only his great barn and one small stall left.

"Me too Lily," he lamented, in a voice now devoid of its customary bull-roaring quality. "I really need to sell the barn too, before my nose rings run out. But who would be able to buy it these days? I can't think of a single horse or cow or sheep or goat who's got those kind of dominos lying around. Seriously, who's going to buy it?"

Who indeed, but the foxes! For the foxes, matters were different than for the majority of the animals. They were in as much a position to buy as ever before, and slowly but surely, almost like winter turning to spring, the prices of certain rare items or especially desirable parcels of land or buildings began to shoot up again. Since Erroll's barn was spacious and well located, one of Blink's young nephews decided it was just the thing he and his friends needed. He bargained hard – pleading poverty even – and Erroll eventually agreed to the sale.

"I've got just enough to stay on in the little stall," he said. "It'll certainly take some getting used to after the comforts of the barn, but I suppose I'm better off than most. And I'm sure that there will be better times ahead."

Merlin, meanwhile, had begun to use some of his surprisingly large hoard of nose rings to buy some choice plots of farmland and a much larger shed to live in. It was less ostentatious than Erroll's barn, and once again fitted out in the restrained style of his earlier shed. But it was a fine property that Merlin hoped he would enjoy in comfort to the end of his days.

Even allowing for the fall in prices, the renewed appetite

the foxes showed for buying and selling sheds and barns bewildered the other animals. Perhaps the good times were surely just around the corner again! Perhaps the Great Winnowing was nothing but an aberration! Hope suddenly rose again in the animals' breasts.

Worse was to come, however. For a long time, no fox had any confidence in what the IOU of his fellow fox was worth, however many paw marks they had on them. However many dominos the Chief Rabbit printed, the only thing the foxes wanted to do with them was to lend them to the pigs, in exchange for more IOUs from the Tithe Barn. For a time, this suited the pigs, since the slump in activity on the farm had led to a corresponding slump in tithes collected, just at the time when virtually every kind of animal was begging for more help. This meant that the pigs themselves had to borrow more, and luckily the foxes were only too eager to lend to them.

But eventually, for no apparent reason, the foxes changed their minds and slowly but surely, the whole carousel of IOUs started up again. What is more, the Forge had been "printing like rabbits", so that when activity started again, it was with a vengeance. The flood of new dominos took almost every animal by surprise, and the prices of almost all items began to shoot up, as the pigs and foxes, and the other animals with dominos began to chase whatever was on offer. This time, however, it was less the sheds and stalls and barns that rose in price, given the lack of confidence in the future which the animals now felt. Rather, the prices of turnips and grains on which the animals relied, and which were being grown in less quantity than before, began to rise. So too did those items brought in from the Great Outside, which were now rarer than before.

Many of the poorer animals began to find that all but the

very cheapest foods were getting beyond their reach, while all but the wealthiest struggled to buy the little luxuries that had made their hard toil seem at least partly recompensed. Apart from the foxes and pigs, only those animals who had hoarded nose rings or had bought land or sheds in good locations which they could rent to those in need, were safe from the ravages of the ever rising prices. If things went on this way for much longer, some of the animals would starve.

So the pigs decided enough was enough, and went to talk to the Chief Rabbit, who thought things over very carefully, all the while chewing on his customary carrot, which was of the plain old-fashioned orange colour.

"The problem, your swineships, is simple," he said, carefully laying in front of him his carrot. "There is just too much paper on Market Farm. So much of it will have to be burned, and replaced with good old fashioned nose rings."

"It is time," he said, pausing for dramatic effect, "for austerity for all."

The pigs did not quite like the sound of this, but they suspected the rabbit was right. The farm had indeed been overwhelmed by too much paper, and it was amazing that until now, no animal had apparently been able to see the problem with such clarity.

While the problem was simple, however, the solution was not. There were, after all, no more nose rings to be found, nor the metal to make them from – indeed that was largely the point. The only solution was to turn to the Great Outside. A delegation of pigs was accordingly dispatched to the neighbouring farms and negotiations began. It took time and the conditions were tough – much of the future produce of the farm for years to come would have to be given in exchange for the metal – but in the end the pigs got what was needed.

Finally, the new nose rings were delivered to the great Central Piggy Bank and the pigs then insisted that the foxes take nose rings in exchange for some of the IOUs they held, so that they could fill up their own piggy banks. The proportion of the exchange did not please the foxes too well, but they saw the determined look in the pigs' eyes and decided that they were better to quit while they were still ahead, especially considering just how very far ahead they were!

But what to do about the return of the nose rings to the farms from the Great Outside, and the produce that had been promised them? Urgent meetings were held between the pigs, the foxes and the rabbits, and it was agreed that the only solution was for all the animals to receive fewer dominos for their labours and to pay much more in tithes each year. The Common Trough would also be cut, as well as the number of animals employed in giving out the corn and turnips. The produce thus saved and the tithes collected would allow the rabbits to gradually burn much of the paper that had piled up, turning the IOUs and dominos into smoke. Not even the Chief Rabbit or the cleverest of the foxes knew how much paper they would have to burn to achieve this, but they knew it would be measured in years, if not decades. In the meantime, the animals – most of the animals that is – would just have to make do with less.

This suited the foxes well enough, since this meant that the many things they owned on the farm, the great stores of nose rings and artefacts they had amassed, would be worth even more. At first, it also mattered little to the other animals, as the small sacrifices they made were little more than a mild additional discomfort. However, the downturn in activity was to prove more painful than even the most prescient among the animals had foreseen. Many of the wonderful and apparently effortless ways of earning a domino had disappeared. Productive fields of the farm had been turned into largely unwanted barns and sheds and huts, so there was less land to farm and fewer animals were needed to work the land. Nor could they graze the common land, for these had all come into the hands of individual animals, mainly pigs and foxes. The lower wages and the increased tithes all began to bite with the savagery of a wolf.

The animals had become used to the years of plenty, and were not inclined to accept that their hard work would result in their being only a little better off than their forefathers. In particular, they suspected that the foxes, however discreet, and the pigs too, were enjoying life much as before the Great Winnowing.

If anything, the anger now seemed more vehement than during the Great Winnowing itself and the pigs made sure that the dogs were more visible and audible.

"After all," as Blink reminded Scratcher. "Keeping the animals content and under control is precisely your job as pigs. Nothing will be achieved if law and order aren't maintained." Although he did not express it so directly, he felt that the foxes had every right to expect to be kept out of harm's way.

Over time, however, the anger simply grew and grew, until finally it boiled over. On one occasion, an angry flock of sheep, who had been shorn so closely that they began to bleed, besieged the Farm House. This time, the protest did not stop at a noisy baaing and bleating. Rocks were thrown and some windows of the Farm House were broken, and pigs were pelted with rotten tomatoes. The dogs appeared in force and, with much barking and bearing of teeth, succeeded in rounding the sheep up and herding them into specially prepared steel pens. Most were let go, but the ring leaders were kept under lock and key, to prevent further disturbances.

Then some chickens walked out of the factory and refused to lay any more eggs, Lily marching among them, proud to be taking destiny under her own wings, and in any case, having literally nothing to lose. Feathers flew and there was a din such as no animal believed a mere flock of chickens could make. In the end, however, confronted in "talks" with an impressive array of foxes, all with their very sharp smiles, the chickens began to waver. The foxes warned darkly of bringing in chickens from neighbouring farms who would be only to glad of the chance to work in such a nice factory.

But then the cows kicked over the milking machines and would not give any more milk and the horses refused to draw any equipment and the sheep refused to be sheared. The entire life of the farm, and with it the ability to pay back the other farms from which nose rings had been borrowed, threatened to grind to a halt. Finally, a march of all the animals was planned on the Farm House and then Vegetarian Villas. The prosperity of the foxes and the rule of the pigs were in danger of being undermined!

Fraught negotiations were held between these recalcitrant animals and the pigs, led by Squeaky, symbolically brandishing a carrot in one trotter and a stick in the other. These lasted for days and sometimes deep into the night. Progress was slow, however, and the talks dragged on for days and weeks.

Eventually, the foxes demanded that firm action be taken. So once again, the dogs were sent in to haul the most troublesome cows and chickens away and put them in the pens, leaving the pigs free to offer a few carrots and seeds to the other animals who accepted them as the price of returning to milking and laying. Lily, for one, was grateful for the seeds, and quiescently returned to the factory.

Market Farm

The foxes once again celebrated in fine style. "The pigs have saved our bacon!" cried Blink in wittily triumphant form at a celebration dinner. Indeed it was just one of many such celebrations in Vegetarian Villas or at the Fat Goose at Play – though they were careful not to let the other animals see their feasting and drinking too much, much less to overhear their conversations.

Plus Ça Change

Several years had passed and it was another quiet day on Market Farm. The pigs wandered about the yard and into the Farm House. The animals went about their work, the chickens to the factory, the cows to the milking sheds and the horses to the fields. In the distance, some foxes were to be seen on their way to Vegetarian Villas.

As the frenetic activity of recent times had receded, all the animals were left wondering how on earth they could have been so busy for so long, and what it had all been for. True, there was a certain nostalgia for the highly-carved turnips and purple potatoes that had marked this extraordinary period in Market Farm's history, and for the sheer giddy optimism – albeit tinged with fear – that had characterised the age. In any case, a small minority of the animals still enjoyed such treats, and on a regular basis.

Difficult, too, was the adjustment most had to make to enjoying less abundance, as if it was simply not the right way to behave to sit and chat with friends, rather than think of new ways that a meadow might be turned to good, speculative use.

Thanks to the prudence, and perhaps good fortune, and certainly generosity of Merlin, Lily and Erroll had managed to escape the worst of the debacle. Erroll continued to work at the treadmills, which in reduced form continued to attract a number of pigs and other animals of substance with their promise of youth and vitality.

"And I have to say," he mused one evening over a fine supper with his friends. "That as I contemplate the porcine backsides of those I am whipping into better health, I'm not always envious of those days when all I could see or think about was the next shed or barn."

Lily had been offered some extra work by Merlin, and free use of a little coop on his small estate, so that over time she was able to repay the nose rings she had owed, and was back to where she had started from all those years ago. She too had accepted her fate. "They were heady times, even for a little chicken like me, Merlin," she cluckled softly, sipping the last of a small glass of elderflower wine. "How I wish I'd listened to you!"

Merlin smiled gently at her, as he refilled her glass. He was not in the mood for anything other than making the most of his good fortune and sharing it with his friends. He had his fine house, his treadmills, the little shops he had bought and he still kept stashed away piles of nose rings against, as he put it, "sunny days when the crops will wither". In other words, he had enough, and was content.

To Merlin's surprise, even the three friends had felt their anger towards the foxes and pigs dissipate over time, despite it being apparent that these animals had increased their possessions even as most of the animals had been forced to sell theirs. This was not the least astonishing of all the events that had occurred.

But the riots had come and gone, and the fury of the herds was spent – and of course many of the worst troublemakers had been safely locked in the steel pens, guarded by the increasingly vigilant dogs. The years of "austerity for all" had allowed many of the dominos and IOUs to be burned, and a token gesture had even been made of making the foxes pay a bit more in tithes each year – though not enough to inconvenience them in any way.

But it could have been worse, most animals thought. They had heard terrifying tales of other farms that had fallen into difficulty, where the dogs had ousted the pigs and had run the farm themselves along strict disciplinary lines. In these farms, every animal had good reason to fear the knock on the shed door in the middle of the night, which would see him hauled away to some dreadful pound to be savaged by the dogs, often for no apparent reason. In one particular farm, the dogs had even sought out each and every rabbit and roasted them in giant ovens. The rabbits, the dogs had argued, had been at the centre of the troubles of every farm that ever was since the beginning of time and to purge them was to save not just their farm, but the whole farm-animal kingdom.

Far better, the animals of Market Farm considered, simply to accept the injustices done and "move forward". There was talk of replanting the Freedom Tree and replacing the plaque saying "prosperity for all", which was now so at odds with all that was happening, with the original that said "freedom for all". But no one could find it. Moreover, the stump where the tree had once stood and spread its shade looked a sorry sight, and the animals who had bought the parts that were sold off wondered what the little bits of wood they now possessed amounted to. Many pieces had been discarded or burned, and altogether the project of a new Freedom Tree seemed beyond even the most energetic animal's reach. So the tree remained a stump, and this in any case seemed an appropriate symbol of all that had passed and a truer reflection of the reality that was Market Farm.